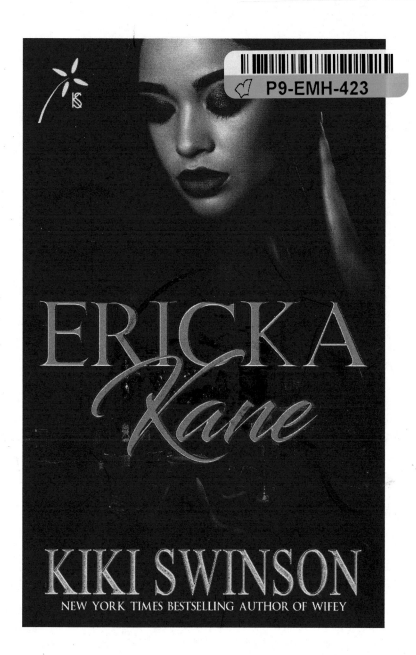

ERICKA *Kane*

KIKI SWINSON

NEW YORK TIMES BESTSELLING AUTHOR OF WIFEY

CH

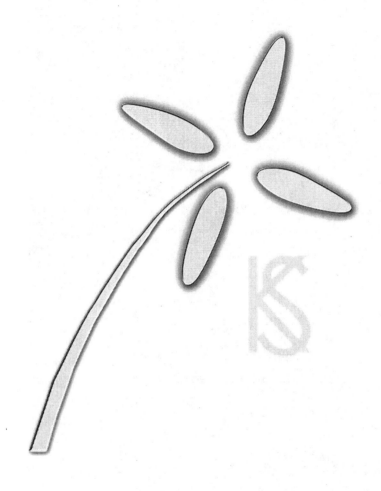

KS PUBLICATIONS
WWW.KIKISWINSON.NET

This is a work of fiction. All of the characters, organizations, and events portrayed in this novel are either products of the author's imagination or are used fictitiously. New York's Finest. Copyright © 2018 by Kiki Swinson. All rights reserved. Printed in the United States of America.

Publisher's address:
K.S. Publications
P.O. Box 68878
Virginia Beach, VA 23471

Website: www.kikiswinson.net
Email: KS.publications@yahoo.com
ISBN-13: 978-0986203763
ISBN-10: 0986203769

First Edition: January 2014
Second Edition: February 2018

Editors: J. Wooden & Letitia Carrington
Interior & Cover Design: Davida Baldwin
(OddBalldsgn.com)
Cover Photography: Davida Baldwin
(OBDPhotography.com)

ALSO IN STORES NOW:

Prologue

My naked body shivered as my blood ran down my face, chest, and stomach. I couldn't stop my legs from shaking. Not to mention, my bladder felt like it would explode at any moment. Wherever they had me, it was literally freezing cold like I was naked in Alaska. "Hit her again," a man's voice boomed. I braced myself because I knew exactly what was coming next. "Please," I whispered, but my words were ignored. It was clear that these were some very dangerous people and they were not going to have any mercy on me. It also became clear that if I ever got out of here alive, I would go on a serious mission to hunt down each and every one of these motherfuckers and torture them ten times worse than they did to me.

"Agggh!" I let out another scream as I felt the shock waves from the oversized stun gun that was being used to torture me. It had to be something they use on large farm animals to make them submissive. I didn't know how many more high-powered surges of electricity my body would be able to take.

My face was scrunched up and my eyes rolled into the back of my head. Sweat was pouring from every pore on my body. I gagged but nothing came up from my stomach. I was in so much pain I felt like even the organs inside of my body hurt. My heart pounded painfully against my weakened chest bone and my stomach literally churned. I was wishing for death because even that had to be better than what I was feeling at the moment. Another hit with the electric current caused piss to spill from my bladder and splash on the feet of one of my tormentors.

"This bitch pissed on me!" he growled. Then he took his huge hand and slapped me across the face so hard spit shot out of my mouth.

"Daddy! Help me!" I struggled to get the words out as my body jerked fiercely from another hit from the stun gun.

"Please let her go," my father mumbled, his words coming out labored and almost breathless. "Just take me, but let her go," he whispered through his battered lips. I had heard him coughing and wheezing as our captors beat him unmercifully. It was almost unreal what we were going through. As hard as the torture was, it was even harder to see my father in a position of total helplessness. He had always been my hero all of my life. When my mother decided that she didn't want to be a mother anymore, it had been my father who'd made all of the sacrifices to take care of me alone. He was always so strong and heroic to me, but now, he was just as weak and useless as me. "Daddy," I panted, my head hanging. "Don't let them kill me."

I squinted through my battered eyes and tried to see him, but the bright lights my torturers were using prevented me from catching a real good glimpse of my father. I figured that I would probably never see him again. I could hear the voices around me clearly though, so I knew we were all in close proximity.

"You betrayed us, Eric. You and your little bitch daughter thought you could outsmart us. I should have never trusted you as a business partner. I should have known that such a weak man, who would run from his native country, would give in to these American ideals. You were once a son of Nigeria...a man who loved his country, now a traitor, a betrayer, and a weak ass man. You got too big for yourself. I knew when you came to this country you would think you were the boss of everything. I let you have a good life here. Yes, you were living in a big mansion, rubbing elbows with the wealthy white Americans that you wished you could call your brothers, and most of all working with the police to bite the hand that feeds you," a tall, ugly man with black skin and yellow eyes hissed as he came into focus in my vision. He had stepped around the bright light and I could see every feature of his hideous face. He resembled a Gorilla because there was something grotesque about his features. His nostrils were almost non-existent and those little beady eyes didn't look like they belonged on a human face at all.

"No. I did everything you asked, Kesso. I was always loyal to you and my entire country and my fellow Nigerians. I helped all of the people you sent to me. I gave them jobs. I gave them money. I gave them places to stay. I repaid my debts to you over and over again. I entered into this business unwillingly, but I did it to repay the debts I owed you for helping me get to America. I turned over everything you asked for…including all of the slaves you wanted. All of the money you wanted, even my wife. You even took the only woman that I ever truly loved from me. What more could I do, Kesso? Now, you have my daughter," my father cried as another round of punches landed in his midsection. More cracks and coughs came as the men pounded on my father, breaking bones and injuring his insides. I heard my father's words, but I couldn't believe my ears. Did my mother run to my father's business partner? Did my father get into something that he would never be able to get out of? It was a lot to handle because I had always worshipped the ground that my father walked upon. My heart was breaking watching him suffer. It was worse than any pain my torturers could impose on me right then.

"Daddy! Stop hurting my Daddy!" It was killing me to know he was in all of that pain. After I discovered what my father was into I was devastated, but that didn't change the fact that I loved him and that he was all that I had in the world. I recognized that the position we were in right at that moment was my fault too. My father had pleaded with me to leave the situation alone. He had asked me to stop investigating and to stop trying to dig up the truth. My father had actually pleaded with me to just accept everything the way it was, but I couldn't do it. He knew how stubborn I could be, but there was nothing much he could do about it. I had to keep investigating for myself. I had to call in the assistance of the police. I wanted justice! That was the stubbornness in me that I had gotten from my mother. She was the type of bitch that never backed down from something that she wanted. As much as I hated her, I was like her in a lot of ways...all of her bad ways. Now, my father and I were facing death with no clear way out of the situation. All because of me! If anyone deserved to die, it was me.

"Daddy I'm so sorry! I just wanted to help. I just wanted to make things better. I just needed some answers. I never meant to have this happen to you. I told you Kesso! Just kill me and let my father go! It is me that you want! I was the one who brought all of the heat to your door and pulled the lid off of your business! It was all me...not my father!" I cried some more. I bet this so-called African prince wasn't used to a woman speaking to him like that. I hated him and I didn't care about any traditions.

"Shut her up! I'm tired of her fucking mouth. This little bitch cost me millions of dollars because she wanted to play Nancy Drew...now I want to see her suffer. She's a piece of shit just like her father. She is not worth sharing the same air with," Kesso, the ugly man barked, waving his hands. His goons immediately surrounded me. My heart rattled in my chest, but there was nothing else they could do to me that would hurt me more than the possibility of my father dying at my hands. I gave up at that moment. Whatever was going to happen must've been our fate from the beginning, I reasoned with myself. I kept screaming things that I knew were disrespectful in the eyes of my father's Nigerian counterparts. I wasn't going to be one of those passive women. No! I knew what those bastards were doing to women and I could only hope that the call I had made before they snatched me would help me in the end.

After a few minutes, one of those huge, wrestler type dudes grabbed me by my hair and dragged me across the gravel floor. "Agh!" I screamed. It was like nothing I had ever felt before. I don't know how I didn't slip into shock after all of those hours of torture I had endured. My entire body felt like someone had doused me with gasoline and lit me on fire. I could feel the once perfect skin on my legs and ass shedding away against the rough floor. I didn't want to die, but if I was going to die, I was going to go out fighting. I tucked my bottom lip under my top teeth and gritted.

"Get off of me! Get the fuck off of me!" I screeched so loud that my throat itched. "Fuck all of you! You're all going to burn in hell for what you're doing!" I continued; feeling blood rushing to places on my body that I didn't know even existed. I bucked my body wildly, but all of my fighting efforts were to no avail. Of course they were stronger than me, which meant that I wasn't going to be able to break free. I never dreamed of going out of this life fighting tooth and nail. My father always called me his little African lion and I planned to live up to that name before I died. The man dragging me finally let go of the fist full of my hair he had been holding. He released me with so much force that my head slammed to the floor. I felt something at the base of my skull come loose. I was dazed for a few seconds, but not for long. I was brought back to reality when I felt a boot slam into my ribs. The force was so great that a mouthful of blood spurted from my mouth.

"You don't have such a big mouth now, huh?" the goon hissed, his accent thick and barely understandable.

"Please don't hurt her anymore. I will give you everything I have if you just let her go," I heard my father gurgle.

"It is too late for that. You and your little troublemaker should've thought about that before both of you betrayed me. Now, someone has to pay with their life. There will be no more talking," Kesso said with finality. The next thing I heard was the ear-shattering explosion of a gun.

"No!!!!!" I belted out, right before my entire world fell apart. Blackness engulfed me and I wondered how it had all come to this. Not even a month ago, my father and I had been so happy.

<u>CHAPTER 1 CELEBRATION</u>

One Month Earlier

"**H**appy Birthday to you…happy birthday to you…happy birthday dear Ericka…" the entire room sang to me in unison. The song was one that I had associated with big expensive gifts and lots of visitors all of my life. My father never let my birthday go by without something big, whether it was a party, loads of gifts or a trip to some far away exotic place. This year he had succeeded in surprising me with the biggest party I'd had since my sweet sixteen and I was elated. It was the best party I had ever had and trust me when I say, I had had some big fiestas.

I smiled so hard my cheeks ached. It was my day and everyone knew it. Even the paparazzi, who was totally obsessed with my family, was allowed to come in and snap a few pictures. That surprised me too, because my father always hated the fact that those aggressive photographers always seemed to catch us at our worst. Flashing lights and those picture thirsty photographers screaming for me to look at their cameras made this event feel like a real celebrity party. Not to mention a few famous faces sprinkled in the crowd. My father had more than one celebrity client and they had come out just for me.

As everyone came to the end of the Happy Birthday song, my father held up his hand and flashed his perfect porcelain veneered smile. He was truly a distinguished gentleman, standing a handsome six foot, three inches tall with a very lean build. Even for his age, my father didn't have those old man guts. He stayed in the gym five days a week and he played tennis on the weekends. He took great care of himself and it didn't go unnoticed. My father wore a very neat salt and pepper speckled goatee, which made his pecan colored skin look rich and smooth. His tailor-made Armani suit and his diamond cuff links screamed wealth. Although he was a second generation Nigerian, my father was mixed with white so his skin wasn't as dark as his other family members. I saw quite a few older and younger women in the crowd swooning over him. My father opened is mouth to speak and captivated the entire room. The crowd that had surrounded my custom made five-tier, Swarovski crystal adorned birthday cake lowered their voices to listen to his baritone. My father could command attention anywhere he went. I always thought he should've gone into politics, but I guess being a native of Nigeria would prevent him from doing that here in the United States. I looked on proudly. Even at his age, my father was hot!

"Good evening everyone. May I have your full attention on this beautiful occasion that we share," my father, the distinguished Nigerian diplomat, Eric Mumbutu, also known in America as Eric Kane, yelled out, quieting the huge crowd. I felt all tingly inside just listening to him. His accent was still noticeable, but not enough to make him seem like he couldn't speak English.

"I brought you all here tonight to help me celebrate my beautiful daughter, Ericka's birthday. It is a bittersweet moment for me, because I can remember the day she was born like it was yesterday. I have sacrificed everything to make sure that my little girl always had the best of everything. I know what it is like to have hardships, so I never wanted my Ericka, my namesake, to suffer any hardships. As of today, she is no longer a baby. She has blossomed into a wonderful woman that has bestowed a great sense of pride to our family name. I am so proud of her and all of the things she has accomplished. At this ripe age of twenty-five she has brought me nothing but joy. To you my daughter, I love you more than life itself and as your father, I will always be here for you," my father beamed, raising his champagne glass high above his head. "Cheers!" Everyone followed his lead. I was on the brink of tears. My father had completely raised me alone after my mother decided that she wanted her own life in Los Angeles. I had never bonded with her, but I had an unbreakable bond with my father. She hadn't even bothered to show up to the party...some social event that she just couldn't get out of was the excuse she used to ditch my party. She had never been a mother to me anyway so I didn't expect much from her.

"Aww daddy! I love you too and I am proud that you are my daddy. Even at twenty-five I will always be your baby girl. I strive to make you proud and keep our family name pure like you always asked," I replied throwing my arms around his neck. My father picked me up off my feet and bear hugged me. The crowd cheered and the sound of glasses clinking filled the air like music. It was one of the happiest moments of my life. My father placed me back on the floor and I couldn't stop smiling. The music picked back up and the crowd began buzzing again.

"Now go enjoy the night. We are paying this DJ and this band to bring you the party of a lifetime," my father joked, planting a kiss on my cheek.

When I turned around the first thing I saw was the beautiful, caramel, smiling face of my best friend, Tia. I rushed over to her, my chest swollen with happiness. She was happy for me I could tell, because she was showing all of her perfectly straight, gleaming white teeth.

"Eww girl, I just love how close you are with your father. And this party right here is just absolutely gorgeous. You will be the talk of the DMV after this. I'm sure it will hit TMZ and all of the other blogs. Your daddy showed you love with this shindig," Tia chimed.

"He really out did himself this time, right? He never ceases to amaze me…that man loves me from here to the moon. I thought it got no better than my sweet sixteen because I had Lil Wayne perform and all of those ice sculptures that night…remember? But this…this is amazing," I said as I looked out on the place my father had chosen—a top notch catering hall that overlooked the Potomac River. The room was decorated all pink and green in honor of my sorority colors. My father had spared no expense. Three-foot tall floral centerpieces with pink and green roses, lilies and hydrangeas sat at the center of all of the tables. The gold chair covers and the beautiful green and pink place settings gave the room a classy air. The five piece live band played original songs my father had composed just for me and he also had DJ Switch, a high profile celebrity DJ spinning music when the band took a break. Each of my guests was going home with a gold bottle of Ace of Spades that had my name engraved on the outside. That alone had to have cost my father hundreds of thousands of dollars. My father had definitely gone all out for my twenty-fifth birthday celebration. I couldn't be more grateful. Seriously, he had me so spoiled I didn't know if any man could ever live up to my expectations.

"I don't know what the wedding is going to look like after this," Tia replied, opening her arms wide. "I still can't get over the hot ass DJ. Do you realize that he plays music for celebrities and he is on the radio for gawd sakes," she quipped. I laughed. Of course I knew who DJ Switch was!

"You know I'm spoiled as hell, Tia. But don't front your father is going to hook you up too next month when you turn the big two five too," I reminded her. Tia blushed because she knew it was true. We were both spoiled rotten from the time we were little girls. We had nothing but the best growing up—private schools, dance, gymnastics, acting classes, equestrian classes, tennis lessons and crew lessons. Sorry to say, none of those things mattered of course because Tia and I just loved shopping, partying and being little social butterflies. We were definitely on equal footing when it came to having things.

"If your father flew that hot ass dress in all the way from Paris for you to wear to my party, you know he is going all out when it's your turn to have a party. He'll probably buy you an even more expensive dress to cover this ass," I joked, slapping her on her thick, round ass playfully. Tia burst into laughter. That's what we did all of the time. We joked, we argued, we shopped, we hung out and we were inseparable most of the time. I couldn't remember one single day not speaking to Tia since we had become friends. Even when we were forced to go on our family vacations overseas each of us would find a way to call one another. I called Tia my Siamese twin. We had each other's backs.

"You're probably right, but still this party is no laughing matter. I had a fucking blast tonight. Honestly, I haven't even been to a club and had as good a time lately" Tia complimented. I hugged her and laughed. The champagne was taking a hold of my

13

senses and Tia's too. She always got real mushy when she was tipsy.

"I love you BFF," Tia said.

"Ditto, chick," I said back.

Tia had been my best friend since we were eleven years old. Both of us came from wealthy families. I met Tia when she moved from France to Northern Virginia. It was an instant friendship. We were two of the very few rich black girls that went to our school; all of the other girls were snobby white girls.

"Come with me to the bathroom. I got something for you. It's the best birthday gift you'll receive all night. Trust me, it's like nothing you've ever had before. You won't regret it at all," Tia yelled in my ear over the loud music. I already knew what it was. That was the one thing that was different about us; Tia had always been way more daring and willing to try new things than I was. She experimented with new drugs almost daily. I wasn't really the type that liked getting high, especially not as much as Tia did. Tia could see the apprehension in my facial expression.

"It's your fucking birthday, don't get scary tonight. Live a little. I shouldn't have to bend your arm to make you feel good. You know you want to get that feeling that we've been chasing since the very first time…c'mon stop acting like you don't," Tia chastised as she grabbed my arm and pulled me towards the clear, mirrored spiral steps that led from the main ballroom to the private bathroom and dressing room suite for the guest of honor.

Tia used her shoulder to push open the doors and she yanked me through the large, gold doors and locked it behind us. Her eyes were wide and she was breathing hard, like what ever she had to show or tell me was really urgent. I never got that excited over drugs. For a quick moment, I wondered if that meant Tia was addicted.

"Ericka, you have to promise to be down with me this time," Tia said almost breathlessly. Sweat was lining up at her hairline making her brassy, blonde hair curl up near her forehead. I crinkled my face. I was always down with my best friend, I just wasn't sure that being down meant trying something that might get me addicted. Getting on drugs was a sure way to make my father die of a broken heart.

"This is some new shit you have never tried. Trust me, premium is an understatement. I got it from my mother's dealer, Cinco. He is sweet on me too so he hooked me up with an extra fat bundle. I'm thinking that he wants to fuck me, but I'm not sure," Tia bragged, putting her exclusive, lavender colored Chanel caviar bag up on the granite counter top. I twisted my lips at what she was saying. Tia was getting into this shit too heavy for me. It had gone beyond experimenting with weed like we had done at thirteen, or sniffing a line or two of coke at a party like we had done at seventeen.

"I didn't like it the last time. I don't know if I'm down with this. You know I'll do anything for you T…but I think you're getting a little too deep with this now. It seems like you are doing this every time we are together," I said apprehensively. Tia rolled her eyes and sighed. I looked at her real good in the light. She was still strikingly beautiful, but she looked like a fiend salivating over drugs right then. I squinted my eyes as she dumped a small mountain of the drug onto the back of her hand. Tia stood almost six feet tall with long, slender legs, a tiny waist, and a flat stomach with large cosmetically placed boobs. Tia's slanted grey cat eyes against her caramel skin and naturally thick, Beyoncé blonde hair made her look like an exotic beauty that should be gracing the cover of Sport Illustrated or some high fashion magazine. She had inherited the best features of her Brazilian father and her African-American mother. I mean, I wasn't a slouch in the looks department either. My skin was lighter than Tia's, almost the color of butter. I guess my father being African couldn't hold up to my mother being white. I had the deepest, darkest, brown eyes and my thick black eyelashes always caught people's attention. My thick, long, hair was naturally jet-black. My personal hairstylist always told me that people would die to have their natural hair color as rich as mine. I was shorter than Tia, but I had a small waist, round hips and an ass to match hers. I hadn't gone under the knife for new boobs yet, but Tia had because her father was a plastic surgeon. That night I wore a banging Nicole Miller mini dress with the entire back out. It wasn't as exclusive as Tia's dress that had been flown in from Paris, but it served me just fine. I was never jealous of my beautiful friend, but I also knew I wasn't as exotic looking and pretty as Tia was. I kept watching her and thinking that if she continued using drugs she wasn't going to be so beautiful for long. "Stop being scary, Ericka. It is still experimenting. I am not addicted if that's what you're trying to imply," Tia retorted. "Now don't be a baby all of your life. Remember you just turned twenty-five yesterday."

"What does my birthday have to do with it?"

"It has everything to do with it. Now watch me work."

Tia placed her nose on top of the mound of happy dust on her hand and inhaled like a high-powered vacuum cleaner. When she finished there was absolutely nothing left on her hand so I was amazed. I didn't even see any residue. Tia was a fucking pro at sniffing lines, obviously.

"Uh!" she grunted as her legs went weak. I thought she would fall, but she just stumbled around all the while keeping her balance. "Whoa! Hot damn!" She shouted and then she started laughing although neither of us had told a joke. Tia was doing some crazy dance. She kicked off her Louboutin heels and jumped around like a white girl trying to dance. It was crazy to watch. After a few seconds, I guess she remembered that it was my turn. Tia went back over to her bag, got the good out and began getting some of the drugs ready for me.

"Ericka...do it! It's my birthday gift to you. C'mon...it'll make you forget all about that dickhead Cyrus," Tia slurred, still laughing without anything being funny.

17

ERICKA *Kane*

When she brought up my ex-boyfriend Cyrus, the hairs on my skin stood up. I felt my heart swell with pain and that was all I needed as a battery in my back. Tia always knew how to tug at my heartstrings and get me to bend to her will. Tia had a small pile of the drugs ready for me.

"Don't be scared birthday girl. Just take it in and forget all of your troubles. It works wonders," Tia whispered like she was my fairy godmother speaking in my ear. I knew better. I didn't have a good gut feeling about it, but I couldn't say no. I swept my long hair aside and bent down, but before I inhaled, I asked, "What is this shit? It's not white; it's like a bluish color. I've never seen anything like this before." The concern was definitely underlying my words. Not that I was going to back down from my strong willed friend, but I had to ask. It was the only stand I would make.

"Yes boo! It is a new blue crystal meth called arctic ice. We are the first people to get our hands on it. I guess that is the perks of being rich bitches. I'm telling you E…you will never be the same after you try this shit. It is not made in some dirty meth lab. This was made in like a full state of the art scientific lab. Only us rich folks can afford even an ounce of this shit right here. Cinco said we could use half the amount and get doubly as high as regular crystal. It's preemo, nothing like that fucking homemade Drano type of shit," Tia explained, giggling the whole time like she was giddy as hell. One thing I must say, the drug was lasting a long time in her system so I knew it was pretty potent. Knowing that made my apprehension about trying it even stronger.

I had always had a hard time telling my best friend no. So, with hundreds of party guests right above celebrating me, I was locked in a bathroom against my better judgment experimenting with God knows what kind of new drug she had gotten her manicured fingers on.

"Let's go Ericka. You're not going to leave me to experience all of this happiness alone are you? Stop being a baby. Get your mind off of Cyrus. Show yourself a good time. Don't walk around with a stick up your ass all of your life. Don't be a daddy's girl forever. Life is for living," Tia kept on prodding and prodding.

"Ok! Ok! Just shut the fuck up! You sound like a damn broken record," I snapped. And finally I relented. Most of the time I just did whatever Tia wanted to do because she was one of those strong personalities that would hound you until you just gave up.

I flared my nostrils and breathed in as hard as I could. Probably not as deep as Tia had sniffed, but deep enough for the little blue particles to fly up my nose. I swear it was like someone had slammed a hammer into my forehead. That blast was powerful as hell.

"Ah!" I stumbled backwards. I immediately threw my hand up over my nose as tears involuntarily danced down my eyes. As the drugs took its place in the membranes of my nose it started to feel like someone had shoved two fire lit sticks up each of my nostrils. The pain radiated all the way up to my brain. Tia was laughing hysterically at my reaction. I was bouncing on my legs and flailing my arms. It was all I could do to keep from screaming in agony.

"Oh shit. What the fuck Tia?" I cringed as I shook my head trying to get the pain to stop. Within seconds my entire body felt different—lighter. The pain subsided seemingly as quickly as it had started. My muscles began relaxing too. Suddenly I was feeling euphoric; I guess this was the extreme high Tia was referring to because the entire room began looking like a rainbow of colors dancing on the walls. I swayed on my legs and my eyeballs moved rapidly without me telling them to.

"You're feeling it aren't you? Ha! I told you this was like nothing we had ever tried before. Fuck that purple kush shit we started off with because this shit here is the new aged stuff. That outer space experience," Tia cheered, elated that I was down with her now. I was feeling light on my feet as the drugs continued to ease my senses. I stumbled around trying to find a chair because I felt like my knees were melting like butter against the sun. I couldn't front there was something superb about the way I was feeling. My skin was even sensitive to the touch. Tia was right. Whatever was in the new blue stuff was unlike anything we had ever tried out before. I didn't want to admit that I wanted another hit, but I think secretly someplace deep down inside, I really did want to suck in another nose full of that shit.

Finally, I slumped down into one of the vanity chairs. Small swirls of colorful lights began clouding my vision. My lips began curling into a smile, but I wasn't telling them to smile. I was kind of aware now that I had no control over my own body parts. I felt like singing and dancing and jumping around. I couldn't move even if I wanted to. I hung onto the chair for dear life because every few seconds I could feel myself slipping off the side. I truly felt like my body was made of jelly.

Tia's mouth was moving but I couldn't hear her. My ears were filled with noise that I had no clue where it was coming from. It sounded like little angels playing instruments around me. I waved my hand at Tia as I watched her dump another small mound onto her hand and in my head I was saying don't do it, but my mouth wouldn't move. I didn't think she needed to take anymore. A quick thought came into my head of my father finding out about our little experiment and a flash of panic flitted through my stomach. I tried to wave at Tia again, but again, my hand wouldn't cooperate with the signals from my brain.

Tia turned towards me and did a little happy dance. Dancing for drugs? Right then and there I knew she had to be addicted. Only drug addicts danced for drugs and got that happy over getting high.

"Ain't no nigga like the one I got...right here this blue ice fucks me better," Tia sang mocking the Foxxy Brown song. I couldn't even laugh at her silly ass. But, I watched as Tia deeply inhaled the second little mountain of the blue stuff in through her nose.

Her reaction was instantaneous. "Oww!" Tia belted out. She bent over at the waist for a few seconds. That's how powerful that shit was—it even made her ass weak in the knees. Then Tia stumbled over to me, took a small amount of the arctic ice meth and placed it up against my left nostril. I didn't want to inhale it, but as soon as I took a breath the drugs disappeared up my nasal cavity. It hit my brain within seconds and more tears danced down the sides of my eyes. This time it didn't hurt as bad but the buzz took me through a vortex of time and reality. Shit started spinning in the room and I felt like I could just fly. My eyes were moving even more rapidly than before. My heart was pounding like I had run miles and miles at top speed. It beat so hard that I could even feel it throbbing in my throat. Sweat poured down the sides of my face. I was sure that my professionally done makeup looked a cakey mess by now.

I watched as Tia spun around in front of me. She was moving like a true drug addict. Like she was speeding. I couldn't move, I literally felt buried alive in my own body. I was screaming and saying things in my head, but my mouth would not move. Tia danced and jumped around for what seemed like an eternity. Finally, she had worn herself down until her body finally collapsed to the floor. My mouth opened but I couldn't scream. I could hear something that sounded like heavenly harps playing in my ears and I suddenly felt like I was suspended in the air over the room. There were a lot of bright lights clouding my eyes. It was so bright I started squinting. My vision and my hearing began to fade away that instant. I could hear my heart slowing down too. The next thing I felt was some unknown force lifting me up from the chair as if I was suspended on a piece of rope. I could feel some cold breeze whipping around me. I remember shivering, but was unable to cover myself with my hands. I didn't know if I was dying or what, but suddenly I was looking down from the ceiling at my best friend and myself. How was that even possible? I was plastered to the ceiling looking at myself in the same room. I felt like throwing up, but nothing came up. I was not inside of my body, which was painfully clear now. Now I know what people meant when they said out of body experience.

From my sudden aerial view, I could see that Tia was sprawled haphazardly on the hard, marble floor of the upscale bathroom. Her beautiful, model like long legs were splayed in an awkward position that looked like it was causing her a lot of pain. Tia resembled a broken Barbie doll that some little girl had twisted into awkward positions and discarded. As for me, as I looked down at myself, I could see that I was lying flat on my back after falling out of the vanity chair. My mouth hung open, my eyes were wide staring straight up at nothing and my hair lay around me like a black death shroud.

"Get up Ericka! Get up and go get help Ericka!" I was screaming at myself but nothing happened. I was stuck on that ceiling looking down, but the Ericka that was on the floor was stiff. I couldn't move from either place. I couldn't call for help because no one could hear a dead girl. I couldn't breathe because that throbbing in my heart had already stopped. I couldn't help Tia or myself. I was powerless and I couldn't find her. I wondered if Tia was with me up on the ceiling looking down at us too. I wondered if she was screaming for help or screaming at herself to get up off that bathroom floor and help her best friend. I wondered if Tia was regretting giving me the drugs in the first place. It was useless trying to figure shit out. I was clearly in a different realm. I didn't know if I was going to be stuck there forever or if someone would eventually find us. This real was one that I couldn't understand then and probably would never be able to speak about again. Tia and I both were either too high to move from the ugly positions we lay in or too dead from an overdose to control what was happening to us. I had probably died at my twenty-fifth birthday party. If that was the case, I was sure that I had probably broken my father's heart into a million little pieces. "I'm sorry daddy. I never meant to hurt you when you were only trying to celebrate me," I said from my position on the ceiling. After that everything went bright white. I am dead. That was the last thing I remember thinking.

CHAPTER 2

Missing

Obviously someone had saved me. Pain was an understatement for the piercing, stabbing and throbbing I felt on every inch of my body when I was finally aware that I wasn't actually dead. I winced as soon as I was conscious enough to feel anything. There was something about bodily pain that had a way of letting you know with one hundred percent certainty that you were alive. I guess you could say that if there was one way to know that you were alive, it was to feel pure pain coursing through your entire body. I couldn't understand why I was hurting so bad though. Had someone beat my ass before saving me? Had I been dragged in order for them to get me up off that bathroom floor? Why God was I in so much pain? I couldn't stop the thoughts from invading my brain.

I slowly opened my eyes, but the daggers of pain that shot through them forced me to snap them shut right away. What had I done to myself?

"Mmm," I moaned and even the vibrations from my moans hurt my lips and throat. I felt someone touch my hand. The contact was warm and sent a warm feeling up my arm. I wasn't alone. This time I fought through the pain and forced my eyes open. My vision was blurry, but I could tell from the silhouette that the person was by my bedside. It was the only person I had expected to be there—my Daddy.

"Ericka, baby, don't ever scare me like that again. Don't you know I would just die if anything happened to you?" my father said softly, squeezing my hand gently. Still groggy and in pain, I finally got my eyes to cooperate enough to look at him. I could see the agony and pain on his face. I immediately felt sick inside. I never wanted to be the thing that brought my father pain and distress. I think my mother had done enough of that over the years. It didn't surprise me that my father was sitting at my bedside alone. Sometimes I believed that my mother felt giving birth to me was probably the worst thing she had ever done in her life. She hated me and she never missed a chance to let me know it.

"Where am I?" I croaked out, my throat was so dry and scratchy it felt like I had eaten a roll of sandpaper. "What happened to me? My body hurts so badly," I barely managed to get the words out.

"At the DC condo. In my room," my father whispered as he reached out and stroked my head.

26

"I'm so glad you're ok. Don't ever do that again. You scared the hell out of me. I don't know what I would do if anything ever happened to you, Ericka. I would have no reason to live," he repeated grimly. I closed my eyes as tears ran out of the sides and dripped into my ears. Hearing his words was enough to break my heart. "How did I get here? What is going on?" I rasped. I had so many questions. It was so weird waking up in a strange place when the last thing I remembered was partying for my birthday.

"Instead of having you go to the hospital and have your name all over the papers, when we found you, I had you brought here and I had my doctor friends take care of you. The hospital was too risky. You would never be able to show your face in public again, I couldn't risk it," my father said. I knew what he was really thinking was that it would've probably brought too much shame on our family name. Africans were big on family names and keeping it pure. I closed my eyes as he spoke.

"Ericka...what were you thinking? This isn't like you at all...to use that stuff. I was shocked when I found out. You were in pretty bad shape, but your prognosis for recovery is good now. Don't you worry; I will have those demons removed from you. I won't let you suffer with them inside of you killing your spirit and ruining your life," my father told me. I crinkled my eyebrows at his words. Demons? What is he talking about? I opened my eyes and looked at him strangely for answers. He returned my gaze, but his look was stern and unwavering. My father was serious about what he was saying.

"Drugs and addiction don't run in our family and I will not have it overtake you. It is a demon. It has to be stamped out of you. You cannot carry our name in those conditions. I have already come up with a plan to get rid of them," he clarified. Sometimes my father's native roots took over in certain situations. This was one of those times. I hardly thought experimenting with a drug was having a demon inside of me. I was too sick and weak and in too much pain to argue with him. If he wanted to call my little mishap a demon, then so be it.

"Daddy, I'm sorry," I whispered, tears draining out of the sides of my eyes. Over the years whenever I got into trouble for things I would say sorry and put on my sad face or shed some fake tears. That usually worked on my father's sensitive side, but half of the time I wasn't sorry for what I had done. This time, I really was sorry. My tears were definitely sincere this time. I knew better that night, but yet I still fell into the peer pressure trap. I had let Tia push my back against the wall. I never wanted him to know that I had even experimented with drugs. "I won't do it again. I promise on my heart and soul," I said sincerely. My words didn't faze my father. For the first time in my life, I felt like my father didn't believe a word that was coming out of my mouth. His jaw was set and his gaze was stony, which made me feel a flash of fear.

"The medicine you were given will take away those drug urges. You will be in pain for a few days because it cleanses your muscles of all traces of the drugs and any ideas of craving them, but you will no longer have the urges. Whatever pain the medicine causes you will endure it and get over this addiction. I had it flown in from Africa, it is illegal here in America, but I don't care. You will not be a drug addict as long as I have breath in my body, Ericka. You will not bring shame to my family and the long line of women who take pride in themselves. Women who take drugs do unsavory things for drugs. Things that I can't ever imagine seeing you do," my father said seriously. I closed my eyes. He was really ashamed of what I had done, I could tell. I mean, we had money so I wouldn't have to do unsavory things for drugs. I guess I couldn't argue with him because he was right, what I had done was stupid and careless. I listened to him go on and on. Little bits and pieces of that night began to come to the forefront of my mind.

Then like a light bulb going off in my head, I suddenly remembered that when I had my mishap with the drugs Tia was there too. Panic came over me like a bucket of ice cold water had been dashed into my face. What had happened to Tia? If I was in bad shape like I was now, what about her?

"Daddy," I groaned. My father stopped lecturing me for a moment and looked at me sympathetically this time. "Ahem," I cleared my throat.

"Yes Ericka?" my father asked, lifting my hand that he was holding in his.

"Where is Tia? Is she ok too? She was with me that night...I remember...we both...is she ok?" I rasped out, trying to sit up despite my back and chest feeling like a huge elephant was sitting on them. It had suddenly occurred to me that Tia had been the last person I'd seen before I blacked out. She had gotten high with me, but did she overdose too?

"Daddy?!" I coughed, the pain hitting me in the chest like a man's fist. My father cleared his throat and moved a few steps away from my bedside. He was avoiding my question. I knew him so well. He wouldn't even look at me. Something was definitely strange about his reaction.

"Daddy...tell me what happened to Tia! I want to know now," I cried out reaching my hand out towards him like someone begging for mercy. My father shot me an awkward look. It was a cross between evil and scared. His eyes glinted in the dim light but something looked vacant about them. My father's reaction told me that he knew something but he wasn't sharing it.

"Is Tia dead?!" I screamed, kicking my sore legs. "Is Tia ok?!" I hollered throwing a tantrum. I was reacting like a true crazy person, but why was my father ignoring me. All he had to do was tell me the truth and I would've accepted it.

"Daddy! Did Tia get out ok!! Did you take her to the hospital?! Where is my best friend!" I screamed like a madwoman. My head was pounding between my ears now. "Daddy!!!!!" I screeched. My father folded his arms and turned his back towards me...something he had never done before.

"Olla! Olla!" he called to our housekeeper. Olla was there in a flash. Her brown face crinkled in confusion.

"Give Ericka some more sedatives now! She can't get herself upset or else that hit she took on her head will be aggravated. They said these hysterics would be one of the side effects of the medication. Take care of her now! I can't have her yelling and screaming like this...penthouse suite or not we have neighbors. I want this screaming stopped at once," my father demanded. He was acting like a shrewd businessman or a bastard. Nothing like the soft, loving, sensitive father I knew. Something was real fishy and it surely didn't sit right with me.

"Yes sir, Mr. Kane," Olla said, shaking her head up and down. She rushed towards the dresser to get something. I kept screaming about Tia, but noticed the needle in Olla's hand.

"No! I don't want to go back to sleep! I just want to know if Tia is ok! Let me have my cell phone so I can call her!" I screamed like a madwoman.

"You will stop this at once," he said through clenched teeth. Then my father forcefully pushed my shoulders down causing me to fall back onto the stack of pillows on the bed. He put the weight of his fit, hulking body over me and with as much pain as I was in fighting him was useless, but I continued to try. I bucked my body wildly, getting almost dizzy from the throbbing pains.

31

ERICKA *Kane*

"Ericka, I demand that you lie down and stop this nonsense! Tia is a bad influence so whatever happened to her, she deserved it. I am responsible for you and you alone! She was the one who brought the drugs to you…I don't want to hear her name right now…not ever," my father growled through is teeth. I could tell by the squaring of his jaw that he was not playing. Olla plunged the needle into my left arm. The pinch from the needle was gone as fast as it came. Every muscle in my body quickly gave in to the tranquilizing drugs. Shit started getting blurry and spinning in the room.

I finally involuntarily acquiesced and relaxed back onto the bed. In my mind I told myself I would sneak my cell phone once my father was gone, but my body had other plans.

"Don't do this to me daddy. Just tell me where Ti…" I slurred, but I never got to finish my sentence. Sleep overcame me like a dark cloud, but even in my dreams I was thinking about my best friend. Her face played on the backs of my eyelids like one of those old fashioned home movies. Tears drained out of the sides of my eyes as my eyelids seemingly glued themselves shut. I was out of it, but I wasn't going to quit. I knew I wasn't going to sleep forever and when I awoke there would be hell to pay. After all, Tia and I were inseparable and not even my father could keep me from finding out what had happened to by best friend in the whole world.

CHAPTER 3

News Flash

66 **I**n breaking news this evening,
Arlington County police are searching
tonight for a missing woman who they
are reporting is Tia Cassidy, the twenty-four year old
daughter of prominent plastic surgeon, the prestigious
doctor Marcel Cassidy. Cassidy and his wife say they
last spoke to their daughter via telephone the night she
went to celebrate her best friend's birthday. Dr.
Cassidy told Arlington police that he and his wife have
a great relationship with their daughter and it is not like
Tia to go away without contacting them. Police have
spoken to a limited number of witnesses so far who say
the young woman was last seen at the posh Waterford
Tower where her parents say she attended her best
friend's birthday party. Police have not revealed
whether or not they have spoken to the best friend or if
Tia Cassidy's late model Mercedes Benz has been

located at this time. Doctor Cassidy and the Arlington police are asking that anyone with information about Tia Cassidy's whereabouts to contact the tip line at 888-MISSING."

I awoke to the sound of the television playing across from my bed. I squinted my eyes and rubbed the sleep away. Olla was on the reclining chair watching the news as she held a vigil by my bedside like my father had instructed her to. At first, when I heard Tia's name on the news and some of the information they were talking about, I thought I was dreaming. More like, I thought I was having a crazy nightmare. But, as I fully came out of my sleep, I listened intently to the reporter's words and quickly realized this shit was real. Unfortunately, it was reality yanking me out of a deep, drug induced sleep. They said Tia was missing and the last place she had been seen alive was my party. Missing? Who my best friend? That fact alone made my heart drop into my stomach. What had I done? Was it my fault Tia was gone? How could she have gone missing, yet they found me? Was she alive? All sorts of thoughts flooded my brain as my body came alive inch by inch and started to move on its own accord. I tossed back the plush blankets and I was out of the bed in one leap. My legs felt weak but that didn't stop me. I moved around frantically until my brain started thinking straight. Maybe I hadn't heard correctly. I wished I could've rewound the news report and took down more details of what they were saying. Olla jumped up from the recliner when she saw me barreling towards her. I quickly noticed that I wasn't in pain anymore and I really felt great compared to how I had felt the day before. I wasn't sure if it was adrenaline or that I was really better, but I didn't care right then. My brain was focused on one thing. I scrambled around the room for my cell phone but it was not there. I probably didn't have to ask why it was missing.

"Olla!!! Olla!!! I screamed at the top of my lungs. My heart was hammering and my entire body felt ice cold. Olla came rushing towards me, her lips white with fright.

"Ms. Kane…please, try to relax," Olla said, her hands out in front of her like she didn't know whether to touch me or not. She probably thought I was having another one of my fits.

"Where is my phone?!" I screamed. Olla spun around like a lost sheep.

"I need my phone now! Tia is missing! I know you heard the story on the news! This is a matter of life and death! I have to speak to someone…get some details…something!" I hollered on the brink of tears. Olla looked like a deer caught up in headlights. She didn't know whether to go left or right. I knew I had kind of abused her over the years whenever I threw one of my tantrums but I didn't know until that day that Olla was really scared of me.

"Olla! Don't just stand there! I need help!" I cried. Tears were coming down my face fast and furious now. "I need my phone because Tia has gone missing. Please," I sobbed.

"I...I...I think your father took the phone yesterday when I gave you the sedatives...so...so that you could get some rest," Olla stammered. Whenever she was scared I could hear her British accent come out. She didn't know whether to go left or right, judging from the way I was acting.

"I need a phone right now. This is a matter of life and death Olla, and I know that you have a damn phone. I was the one who got my father to give it to you...remember? Now give it to me!" I demanded, sniffling back a nose full of snot. Olla looked lost, but she reached into the pocket on the bib of her uniform and pulled out her cell phone.

"Here Ms. Kane. But, please don't tell your father that I allowed you to use mine. He forbid me from allowing you to have a phone," Olla said, extending her cell phone towards me with her hands shaking. With my hands also shaking frantically I snatched it. I punched in Tia's number so fast that the phone misdialed the first time. "C'mon Tia...answer."

"Hello? Hello?" I shouted into the phone, but a loud signal came through letting me know I had not dialed right. "Shit," I huffed. I inhaled deeply and took my time dialing the number the second time. Within a few seconds Tia's voice filtered through the receiver.

"Hello," her voice came through all cheery. "Hello?"

"Tia!" I screamed.

"Sike!" Tia's voice said playfully. Next I heard Tia's annoying schoolgirl, playful laughter come through the receiver. It was her voicemail that she had set up to make people believe it was her answering at first. Once you got caught by Tia's prank you could hear her laughing. "Haha. Got you. I'm not available for any lame calls so leave a message at the tone or don't...suit yourself," Tia's voice message chimed. By the time I got to the end I was burning up. If Tia were in front of me at that moment I probably would've choked the shit out of her.

"Fuck! Tia! Where are you!" I growled, wishing I could throw Olla's phone against the wall. I listened for the dreaded beep on her message.

"Tia it's me Ericka. I don't know where you are but you need to call me as soon as you get this message. No bullshit. No games. Call me," I relayed frantically into the phone. I waited until her voicemail automatically disconnected me. I wanted to keep calling over and over again although I knew Tia wasn't going to answer. Olla was watching me like a hawk, but she was also keeping her eye on the door to make sure my father didn't come and catch me on the phone. Finally, I dropped the phone back into Olla's hand and I slumped back down on the bed. I was overcome with grief. I couldn't even begin to think of what to do next. The only person who would probably know what to do was my father.

"Olla...I need my father. I need him right now because Tia is missing and I think it may have happened after my party. So please, Olla call him right now, I can't deal with this alone," I sobbed.

ERICKA *Kane*

Ericka Kane

Kiki Swinson

Chapter 4 – Mysterious Bullshit

My father arrived looking just as frantic as I had been when I first heard that Tia had gone missing. Maybe he was frantic for a different reason, but he had convinced me at that time that he was just as concerned about Tia as I was.

"Daddy!" I cried as soon as I saw his face. I ran straight into his arms. My father grabbed me into a comforting bear hug. I cried into his chest.

"Oh baby girl, I'm so sorry," my father said as soon as he saw and felt how much pain and grief I was in.

"Daddy! I was the last person Tia was with. I need to know what happened when you found us in that bathroom. Please tell me every minute of what happened," I begged. I had been wrecking my brain trying to remember, but nothing at all came to mind. The entire scene was a blank for me.

"Shhh. Ericka you need to rest. If you get yourself too upset you will get sick," my father comforted as I sobbed like someone had just died. He was clearly avoiding the topic, which struck me in an odd way but I was too upset to even point it out.

"No. I need to find Tia. I need to help with any information I can provide. I have to contact the cops or somebody who can help us find her, "I said sniffling and almost choking on my tears. "Tell me daddy...when was the last time you saw Tia? You found us in the bathroom and then what?" I asked, looking up into my father's face. He lowered his eyes and looked at his feet. That wasn't like him. My father was always a look-you-in-the-eye type of person so his behavior was kind of unnerving to me. I couldn't focus too much on that though, answers were more important to me.

"Ok...ok," he said. "When we found you both, Tia was ok. She was a little dazed from whatever she took, but she was able to come around with a little cold water and some slaps to the face. You, on the other hand, were in worse shape than she was. I had to have you rushed here with doctors in tow to make sure you came through it. I had them help Tia get it together. She was a little too high to drive herself home, so I called a driver. One of the drivers from the service took her home. He assured me that he dropped her off at her apartment in Arlington and watched her go into the building. After that, we have no idea what happened to her, but we did make sure that she went inside her building. That's all I can tell you. I am really sorry she is missing, but knowing her wild lifestyle she is probably gone off with some drug dealer getting high out of her mind," my father told me. I resented him for saying things like that about Tia. She would've never abandoned me.

"But why didn't you just let her stay with me? Why didn't your driver take her all the way to her door and make sure she got inside?" I asked through sobs. Things just didn't add up. My father was really big on protecting women so why would he just discard her like that.

"Ericka my focus was on saving your life that night. Like I told you, she must've taken the drug before because she came around much faster than you did. I didn't know if you would live or die...I wasn't thinking about if Tia was going to go off and come up missing. I had no idea something would happen to her...if that is even the case. When I hire a driver, I can't make him take a passenger to their door. I'm sure they will find Tia and she will be ok. Like I said, she is probably out with a man and will turn up safe and sound," my father said, trying his best to comfort me. I guess he kind of had a point, but I was still miffed by Tia's absence.

"It's just not like her not to call me. I speak to her everyday. I have a really bad feeling about this daddy. I'm telling you, something has happened to her," I replied, my words coming out strong and sure. My father pulled his arm from around me and plopped down on the chair. He pinched the bridge of his nose like he always did when he was contemplating his next move.

"I will find out what happened to Tia if it's the last thing that I do," I said, determined. "There is something that is definitely not right and I am just the person to find out. I don't care what I have to do, Daddy. If someone is responsible for Tia being missing I will find out and I will make sure they suffer," I said with finality. I could've never known then that I was speaking my fate into existence. My father fell silent. We sat there for the next half hour in silence, both of our minds whizzing in opposite directions. The first sign of how split our lives would become.

When the detectives showed up at our condo in DC early the next morning, I could barely open my eyes wide. I had cried for so many hours over Tia that my eyes were swollen almost shut. Her parents hadn't answered the hundreds of calls I had placed to their home phone. I had also tried Tia's home phone and cell phone at least sixty more times. My father had stayed by my side, but I noticed each time I asked for my cell phone to check for any calls from Tia, my father would avoid the topic. He finally came up with a story about my cell phone being at his house because he wanted me to rest. My father had tried several times to get me to take more sedatives, but I wanted to stay awake and alert just in case any more news came out about Tia's whereabouts.

The arrival of the detectives was a welcome distraction and I was hoping and praying they were going to be able to tell me something about Tia's whereabouts.

"Good day, Mr. Kane, Miss Kane," a tall, bald white man nodded as he was led into the den by Olla. I stood up with my arms wrapped around my body. Suddenly I was freezing. I couldn't stop my teeth from chattering. I looked at the two men expectantly.

"I am detective Bowles and this is my partner detective Froch, we came to speak to you sir and you ma'am about the disappearance of Tia Cassidy, who we understand is close to your family and may have been last seen with you all," the other tall, fully grey haired white man announced.

I lifted my head up and looked at the detective pitifully and before my father could say anything I lost it. My legs went weak and I bent over at the waist like someone had gut punched me.

"Please find her! Please find Tia! It's not like her not to call me! I know she had some problems, but you have to find her! She would never leave without telling me where she was going! Something is wrong!" I screamed and cried hysterically. I fell to my knees. "Something is wrong…I just know it," I sobbed.

Both detectives looked stunned by my outburst. My father looked embarrassed and angry at the same time. I didn't care what any of them thought of me. I was in a lot of pain.

"Olla, stay with Ericka while I go speak with the detectives outside of the room," my father said, his tone annoyed.

"No! I want to know what is going on!" I screeched.

"Ericka! Stop! I will find out what they have to say and I will tell you. I promise. Now pull yourself together. This behavior is not helping anything," my father snapped. He never really raised his voice at me unless the situation was really bad. I could tell he was holding on to the last bits of his composure when it came to this situation, and me so I backed down. I knew my father was ashamed and God forbid I brought any shame to our family name.

The detectives followed my father out of the den to the other side of the condo. The anticipation was killing me, but I had already decided I wasn't going to depend on my father or those detectives to find out what happened to Tia. Whatever they discussed did not take long. My father returned with the detective's business cards and tossed them into the small garbage can at my bedside.

"What did they say?" I pressed as soon as my father sat down.

"They want to speak with you tomorrow, but I told them I would have to have my attorney present. They are trying to blame you for Tia's disappearance Ericka. I knew we couldn't trust them. We just have to protect ourselves at this point," my father said gravely.

"Me? Why would I even be considered a suspect? I love Tia with all of my heart. Her parents knew that I would've never done anything to hurt Tia," I said, my voice trailing off. "It wasn't me, but I'm surely going to find out who it was," I said. Things just didn't add up. I felt like the only way I was going to find out the truth was if I got from under my father's eyesight. I closed my eyes and began hatching a plan to get out of the condo without my father and Olla finding out. I knew the only way I was going to find Tia was to hit the streets and start investigating on my own. The first thing I needed to do was to go see her parents. I needed them to know that I would've never had anything to do with Tia's disappearance and that I wanted to find her probably more than they did. I was on a mission. If the cops and my father didn't want to help me, I was going to help myself. No matter what I was going to find Tia.

As soon as my father left the DC condo for a business meeting, I snuck out. Well, I didn't sneak, it was more like I threatened Olla and told her that if she called him or told him I was gone I'd tell him how she had been skimming off the grocery money and using his credit card for personal shit which I had caught onto a while back. I didn't get any protest from her. I got dressed in an all black Juicy sweat suit, pulled my hair into a tight bun, threw on the biggest darkest shades I had at the DC condo and then I left. Olla had given me a little look as I walked out the door so for good measure I told her that if she called my father I would make sure she was sent back to London as a homeless pauper, the same way she had come to America. Olla knew better than to fuck with me so I knew I had some time before my father returned, especially if he thought I was on lock down under Olla's watchful eye. I couldn't take my car because I figured my father would even have our parking attendants looking out for my damn car too, so I opted for a taxi, which I had to catch on the street. That was unheard of for me. I had never hailed a cab for myself in my damn life. I guess I was learning the hard way that there was a first time for everything. I was a ball of nerves during the entire ride. I had flashes of some of the good times Tia and I had shared. Like the time we snuck out of her house to go to a party at Howard University and when we came back we almost got shot by her father's paid security because they thought we were intruders. Tia's parents were so mad at us, but after they sent us to her room we spent the entire night laughing uncontrollably. We fell asleep in our clothes and all that night. There were so many fun nights like that for us. Although I was smiling at the memories when I looked up into the taxi rearview mirror, I immediately felt overwhelmingly sad at the possibility that I would never see my best friend again.

CHAPTER 5

What Will They Think?

W hen I arrived at the Cassidy home, I gasped and my stomach started swirling. I had never seen so many media trucks in my life. There were reporters from at least eight networks camped outside of the huge, black, wrought iron gates that surrounded Tia's parents estate in Potomac, Maryland. When my taxi pulled up, I was trying to figure out how I would navigate through the sea of reporters to get to the intercom box. I knew that Tia's parents' would have their house under strict lockdown with her being gone and so many strangers lurking. I placed my oversized Gucci shades back over my eyes, said a silent prayer and exited the taxi. As soon as I walked up to the intercom box, the reporters descended on me like a pack of lions on a small prey. I mean they were so close to me the hairs on the back of my neck stood up. My hands were shaking as I rang the buzzer on the intercom. I could hardly hear anyone answer because the reporters were yelling things like

"Miss, Miss…are you related to the missing girl" and "who are you? Did you come to tell the parents that you have information about their daughter's whereabouts?" They were screaming and shoving microphones in my face and hovering closely. My head immediately started pounding. Maybe my father was right? I had come out too soon and under these circumstances it wasn't good for me. I was so overwhelmed I felt like covering my ears and running in the opposite direction, but if I had done that I would not have been able to hear the voice coming from the intercom asking me who I was.

"It's Ericka…Ericka Kane, Tia's best friend!" I screamed into the box. The reporters went wild with that little tidbit of information. Then they started screaming stuff like "You were the last person to see Tia Cassidy…what kind of drugs were you taking?" and "Did you and your family have something to do with Tia's disappearance?" Their line of questioning took me aback. How would they know drugs were involved? Why would they think my family or I would have anything to do with Tia's disappearance? My mind was racing in a zillion directions and my body felt tense and rigid, as I stood surrounded by those hounds. I had to wonder if Tia's mother and father had called the reporters themselves because the entire Cassidy family had always been looking for their little fifteen minutes of fame. When we used to go out, Tia would place a call to the paparazzi herself and have them following us around. She was always wild like that and her mother had even tried out for a reality show called Doctor's Wives, but was cut from the show for some reason that I still didn't know until this day.

Within a few minutes of me ringing the intercom four huge, men-in-black, dark shade wearing, wrestler type of security guards arrived at the gate. They were scary but they were also focused in on me. It was like I didn't even have to identify myself, like someone had already showed them a picture of me so they already knew who I was. One of them used his finger to direct me to the opening of the gate. Then another guy who resembled the wrestler the Rock slowly opened the gate a crack to allow me to slip inside. I saw the guard that was standing aside with his hand on his waistband like he was ready to pull a gun out at any second. Is it that serious? Who do they expect a mass murderer? I was thinking to myself. Just as the gate closed behind me I heard it.

"Miss Kane! Miss Kane! Did you come to apologize for what has happened to Tia Cassidy? Did you murder her because you were jealous?" The words caused a cold chill to shoot down my back. There was something about that theory that made me purely sick. The reporters were still going crazy behind me. They were screaming more outrageous questions and two of them even tried to slip through the gate behind me. One of the broad shouldered security guards tossed the two reporters aside like rag dolls. I had to shake off the dreadful feeling that was filling my body. Once I started to get away from that gate and those hateful ass reporters a hot flash of relief washed over me. Once I was inside of the familiar gates, I kind of felt like maybe I would get some answers about Tia. I must admit, it felt eerie and kind of crazy knowing that Tia wasn't there. Since she had gotten her own place in Arlington I hadn't visited her parent's home that often anymore, but whenever I did, it was always with Tia right by my side. She would always say the same thing as we took the long walk up from the circular driveway to the front door. "Be ready to deal with these two neurotics. Don't answer any of their questions and just smile and nod if they ask you any." Hearing Tia's usual warning play in my ears now made a huge lump in the back of my throat. Tears sprang up to my eyes, but I fought to keep them from falling. I didn't realize how much this trip was going to drive home the reality that my best friend was really gone.

"Any news? Has Tia come home?" I asked the guards as they walked me up to the front door of the Cassidy mansion. The guards were eerily silent. I felt like I was walking with robots or androids from some futuristic movie. They didn't even acknowledge that I was speaking to them. I guess that's what they had been instructed to do. I wanted to tell them off, but I didn't want to get thrown out before I could even get some answers.

Once I arrived at the main mansion doors I felt a little weak in the knees. I guess my nerves were starting to get the best of me and my mind was definitely playing tricks on me. What if they had already found Tia dead and I just didn't know about it yet? What if Tia was inside having a drink and waiting to surprise me? What if…. I couldn't control these unwanted thoughts from continuously invading my brain. Finally, I was inside the house. Nothing had changed about the very grandiose air of the Cassidy house. Tia's mother was always one to believe the gaudier something is the more it screamed wealth. That could explain the ten huge Austrian crystal chandeliers that spanned the length of the entire first floor of the home. Not to mention, the thick, rich gold Italian silk curtains that adorned the huge custom floor to ceiling windows throughout the downstairs. I dare to mention the floors. I was led through the huge, gold and white marble foyer but how could I ever forget Tia telling me that some of the specs of gold in the marble were real fourteen-karat gold plated specks. As I passed the spiral staircase that led up to the bedroom suites I noticed a new hand painted portrait of Tia hanging on what the Cassidy's referred to as their "grand wall." Tia was not smiling in the portrait but her eyes seemed to hold so much information. Tia had of course struck her most daring model's pose in the painting. It made me smirk as I had a quick thought about how self centered and egotistical my best friend was.

I was led into what I would call the Cassidy library; however, Tia and her family call it the study. The smell of old wood and cigars quickly assailed my nose and hit me in the gut. It felt like little people were standing in my stomach mixing up a witch's brew. My stomach made a loud growling noise that could've awoken the dead. I guess that was the first time I realized I was starving. I knew this place to be where Tia's father usually took care of his business so the scent of the Cuban cigars he smoked didn't surprise me, but it still made me gag. When I walked in Dr. Cassidy was standing with his back turned, his hands shoved deep into the pockets of his pants and he stared out of the huge floor to ceiling window that was behind his grand mahogany desk. The scene was like something out of a mob movie and I kind of felt like I was going to see the Godfather to be admonished for some wrong I had done. My heart felt like it was bouncing around inside my chest. I swallowed hard. What would I say to a man I knew was probably broken into a million pieces over his daughter? I recognized that Tia was the apple of her father's eye just like I was. The difference was that Tia had both of her parents and I only had my father. Sometimes it hurt me when Tia and her mother would do things together. I couldn't think about my jealousies now. I was on a mission.

"Miss Kane has arrived, sir," one of the guards announced. That shit felt like an old world movie where someone announces your presence to a king. With that, the four of security guards stepped back leaving me front and center alone. Dr. Cassidy turned around slowly. He had moved his hands from his pockets and now his arms were folded across his chest. I didn't know what I expected him to look like given the circumstances, but I knew right away I hadn't expected what I saw. Doctor Cassidy's eyes were swollen and red-rimmed, which I could see from a distance so I knew it had to be bad close up. Worry lines creased every inch of his face and his cheeks were drawn in as if he was sucking them into the center of his mouth. I blinked rapidly trying to get a quick mental note of how Dr. Cassidy looked the last time I had seen him. I would've imagined it wasn't like this. He looked like he had aged ten years over night.

"Ericka, thank you for coming," Dr. Cassidy said, his voice sounding feeble like an old man's. With his sad facial expression and his shaky words the tears finally fell from my eyes. I rushed over to him.

"I'm so sorry. Please tell me what is going on? I need to know what happened to Tia. It's not like her to just leave and I don't know what happened to her," I pleaded. Dr. Cassidy set his jaw and looked at me strangely.

"You were the last person to see her at your party that is all we have been told. Your father had said he sent Tia home with a driver, but why would he do that? She was our baby girl, if the tables were turned we would have seen to it that you were returned safely," he said with his voice filling with grief.

"But...but...you don't understand. My father had to save my life. He said Tia was ok. Tia and I were at my party and she had this...this...new drug and...then..." I started rambling, trying to explain and trying in earnest to defend my father. I already knew that the story sounded bad, but I wasn't going to let anyone put the blame on my father or me for what had happened. Dr. Cassidy opened his mouth like he was about to say something, but he never got the chance.

"How dare you come in our house and accuse my daughter of bringing drugs to you!" A shrill woman's voice came from behind me. Even Dr. Cassidy looked shocked. I whirled around so fast I almost toppled over. It was Tia's mother.

"You have the audacity to bring your smug, disgusting presence into our home where we are grieving and holding vigil for our missing daughter and speak about her in that way?!" A deep, grating female voice accused from behind us. Dr. Cassidy's eyes went round and my mouth kind of dropped open.

"You want to blame my Tia for having drugs when we all know you're the one who is on drugs! You're a drug addict and I should've kept my baby away from you the day I found out the types of things you were into and the types of people you were hanging around," Mrs. Cassidy hissed as she came towards me with an accusing finger jutted in my direction. My mouth was full open now but the words just wouldn't come. Talk about at a loss for words and feeling like you had just been gut punched. Mrs. Cassidy let out a crazy cackle that reminded me of a witch or some schizophrenic person. Then she continued her tirade against me.

"Oh now you're speechless? You are a piece of trash! You lured my daughter into things that she would've never dared to try if she hadn't been a loyal friend to you. Oh yes…yes…I know all about you little missy. You think Tia didn't keep me informed about how you experiment with all types of different drugs?"

"What?!" I said. I was shock to know Tia's mom knew as much as she did.

"Don't what me!" she roared. "I know about your drug dealer named Cinco that you sleep with for drugs…oh yeah little miss Ericka Kane or should I say miss cocaine…I know all about you. Tia had tried countless times to help you get off drugs. She told me about the nights she stayed up with you trying to help you detox off drugs. Oh and that trashy party your father threw for you…why do you think we didn't come? Tia had to practically beg us to let her go?" Mrs. Cassidy spat. She was in my face, almost nose to nose with me. I couldn't believe my ears. I felt like someone had actually slapped me across my face with an open hand each time Mrs. Cassidy hurled another accusation in my direction. The things she was saying sounded so ludicrous to me that I had to make sure that I wasn't waking up from a bad nightmare. Detox? Up all night? Tia? Me? Party because I was in rehab? What the fuck type of shit was Tia telling her parents? Obviously Tia had been lying to her mother and to me for that matter. She had definitely told me that Cinco was her mother's drug dealer. Tia had even cried on my shoulder about how her mother's drug addiction was getting so bad that she feared her mother would overdose one day. But why? Why had Tia lied to both of us like that? I guess my theory about her being addicted was true and she knew that the two closest people to her—me and her mother—would have figured her out. Tia needed to create a smoke screen to cover up her own drug addiction. Things were getting stranger by the minute with this thing. Now I was a true believer that Tia was probably dead or in more trouble than I could've ever imagined.

I started to say something to defend myself against Mrs. Cassidy's vicious verbal attack, but I thought better of it. After all, the Cassidy's were grieving for their daughter so what good would it have done for me to throw Tia under the bus.

"Now, unless you came here to confess to us just what you did to Tia you get out of here and never come back! We will not have the likes of you around us or our property. You're lucky I haven't gotten up enough evidence yet to have you prosecuted, but when I do you will feel the wrath of the Cassidy family. When my daughter is found...whether she is dead or alive you will never see her again. I always knew Tia was too good to be associated with a motherless, immigrant's child like you. Now you leave my home at once. We don't ever want to see you again unless its in the handcuffs you deserve when the police get to the bottom of what you really did to our baby," Mrs. Cassidy growled. It was really strange to hear her speak to me like that after years of her so-called feeling sorry for me and acting like she was my mother after my own mother had abandoned me. Now, a woman I had trusted and loved was hurling insults at me that could've buckled my knees. Her words burned through me and I felt a wave of nausea come over me that I didn't expect. Before I could respond to her in any kind of way the security guards were back to forcefully escort me out. I felt a sense of desperation that I hadn't felt since the day my mother told me she was leaving for good. I had grabbed onto her and tried to keep her from leaving, but that cold, callous bitch wrenched my arms from around her waist, turned swiftly on the balls of her feet and stormed away to her waiting car. I had screamed after her. I was only a little girl, but it was all for nothing. I remember being inconsolable like I was right now, feeling like the entire universe had just toppled down on my head for no reason at all.

"Dr. Cassidy…wait! Let me speak to you! It's not true! None of it is true! You will never get to the bottom of it unless you get the real truth! I have to explain what really happened! Tia might be in danger if you don't listen to me! I think Tia was the one with the drug problem! She was the one with a drug dealer named Cinco! Not me! Tia was the one on drugs!" I screamed as they dragged me away.

"Get that horrible girl out of my house at once!" Mrs. Cassidy screamed. It was like she didn't want to hear what I had to say. Like she was too afraid that the truth would come out. A dark feeling of suspicion crept up on me, but I kept yelling that Tia was the one with the drug addiction. I think it was something Mrs. Cassidy already knew was true. And if I knew her like I thought I did, I wouldn't have put it past her to want to get her daughter out of the picture before Tia's habit became the talk of Mrs. Cassidy's elite social circle. Maybe that bitch had done something to her own daughter.

"Dr. Cassidy! You need to know the truth!" That was the last thing I was able to say. I caught a quick glimpse of his eyes before I was tossed out. Tia's father looked like he wanted to hear what I had to say, but instead of standing up to his bitch of a wife, he slid his arm around his sobbing wife's shoulders and pulled her close to him. All was lost there. I had known for years who really wore the pants in the Cassidy family and it surely wasn't Tia's father. How could they think I would've done anything to Tia? They had known me for years. More importantly, how could Tia have told so many lies? I was itching to solve the mystery of Tia's disappearance even more now. The suspect list was growing in my mind by the minute too. Tia had been her own worst enemy with all of her lies, but I still needed to find out what had happened to her. I knew the first place I had to go in order to search for answers too.

CHAPTER 6

Secrets & Lies

The ordeal at the Cassidy home was one that I wouldn't soon forget. There was just something about a woman yelling things at you like "motherless immigrant's child" that would probably stay with me forever. It made thoughts of my mother invade my psyche like it hadn't in years. My mind wondered if my mother ever thought about how it was for a young girl to grow up without her mother. I know I'd never want to experience that. To grow up without a woman's guidance on her first bra, first period, first love and all of the firsts things that a mother is supposed to share with her daughter would make a young girl feel empty inside. Now add the part where your family disowned you because you married someone from another country. My mother was dealt a fucked up hand.

As I got a bit older that my mother's family hadn't liked the fact that she had married an African immigrant. My heartbreak over my mother would probably never go away and right there in that taxi cab as I headed to solve the mystery of my best friend's disappearance I promised that I would take a trip to Los Angeles and confront my mother about everything she had done to me.

When I arrived at Tia's building in Arlington, Virginia I was feeling a rush of emotions. So much of a rush that I felt like I had really gotten high like I had that night Tia gave me the drugs. My head swirled with a mixture of anger, heartbreak, disappointment, betrayal and anxiety. I mumbled to myself because the thoughts going through my head were just too much to keep inside. Confusion was the biggest thing for me at that moment. "How could she? Why did she? She really wanted me to look bad?" I mumbled to myself as I walked up to the beautiful beveled glass doors of Tia's exclusive high-rise building that sat situated just feet across from the Pentagon.

Tia had painted me as the worse scum of the earth to her parents all along, which told me that her addiction was probably way more serious than I could've ever thought. Of course it was just easier to make me out to be the pitiful drug addict so that her mother and father never thought to look at their own daughter as she changed drastically right before their own eyes. I guess the lies Tia told me hurt worse than knowing she told lies on me. The crafty way she flipped everything around on me was the typical Tia I knew all to well. She'd do anything to take the spotlight off of herself when she was up to her old tricks. Any other time, Tia lived and breathed for the spotlight to be on her. What I didn't understand though is I never asked Tia a million questions. If she were just experimenting like she always liked to refer to it, then why would she tell me Cinco was her mother's drug dealer and tell her mother he was mine? I immediately wanted to know more about this Cinco person. Shit, maybe he had something to do with Tia being missing. Tia was slowly but surely shaping up to be a liar and a sneak in my mind's eye. First sure sign of a real problem is when people taking the drugs start keeping secrets and telling lies. I think Tia had surpassed that stage by a long shot and I had missed the shit totally.

"Hi Preston," I waved to Tia's doorman. He looked at me strangely and then stepped into my direct path, hindering me from going forward towards the elevators. Oh boy! Not you too with the bullshit! I screamed in my head, but for outside appearances I put on the fakest, happiest, smile I could dig up at that moment.

"Um...you do know that Miss Cassidy is not here. I'm sure you've heard about the unfortunate nature of why she is not here," Preston said, his face stony. I could hear suspicion underlying his words. I wanted to fucking curse him out on the spot. Did he know who he was talking to? He wasn't a fucking cop. He was a doorman. Something inside of me was starting to snap apart. I needed to get upstairs to Tia's apartment and I didn't need this asshole trying to stop me. I choked back down the words I wanted to tell this prick and I continued to will myself to keep calm. You can get more bees with honey than with vinegar. I pep talked myself.

"Of course I know that Tia is not here. She is my best friend in the whole world, but I guess you know that Preston. I'm here to get some of her things for her parents. They're too upset to come by. You've seen me a million and one times here with Tia and without her. She is like my family so this is not at all strange," I lied on the spot. My left foot began involuntarily tapping against the floor and my right fists curled up by itself. If this bastard tried me I was going to punch the shit out of him and make a run for it. Calm down Ericka...calm down...calm down. I had to silently talk myself through this mini interrogation before I drew too much attention from other residents coming and going. I couldn't risk anyone calling the police on me. That would've fucked up all of my plans.

"This thing with Tia has everyone upset. Really Preston, I just want to get in and out like I planned," I said as calmly as I could.

"So...so they gave you a key?" Preston asked like it was the most outrageous thing he'd ever heard. I could've slapped the shit out of him, I swear to goodness.

"What do you think? I'm going to just morph through the door? Please Preston, this thing with Tia is upsetting enough. I don't need you blowing it for me today. Now if you'll move out of my way and let me get to my business I won't take up anymore of your time since you've certainly taken up enough of mine," I snapped and then I pushed him out of my way. I was waiting for his ass to say something else but I guess I had left him speechless. My nerves were on a wire's edge. I slid into the elevator and pressed 10. I closed my eyes, took a deep breath and prayed that Tia's extra key was where she always left it. I quickly remembered the first time I found out where she kept that key. It was so funny; Tia and I were blasted out of our minds that night from taking shots with these two so-called baller dudes from New Jersey that night. Tia had been so drunk she couldn't even get her Hermes Birkin bag opened to get the keys out. I was too drunk to figure it out too. So, we had both plopped down on the floor in front of Tia's door cackling with laughter. "I gotta pee pee," Tia had announced which had caused another wave of uncontrollable laughter between us. That wave of laughter had also caused Tia to piss all over herself. "Oh shit," she had slurred. "I know where a key is," she said in her totally hammered voice. Then she got on her knees and crawled down the hallway and retrieved the key. I was laughing and looking at her like she was crazy but her ass had surely come back with a damn key to her apartment. "Nobody would ever think to look there for a key to my place," Tia had slurred that crazy night. From then on I knew where she'd kept her spare key in case we were ever so drunk we were locked out again or like now, in case I had to go into her place in an emergency to help locate her after she'd gone missing.

When the elevator doors dinged open the happy thoughts of the past quickly faded from my mind. I rushed through the elevator doors and sped down the long, carpeted hallway that led to Tia's apartment door. The hallway was pin drop quiet as usual. In a ritzy building like that it was the norm. Although it was quiet and empty, I looked around like a burglar about to rob someone's house that was how nervous I felt. I don't know if I was nervous about getting to the key or nervous about what the hell I was going to find on the other side of the damn door. Shit was coming out about Tia that I didn't know if I liked so far.

I finally made it to Tia's door. I looked down the hallway to make sure the coast was clear. I turned around and walked to her neighbor's door that was two doors over. Tia had told me on many occasions that the occupant of that apartment was an old man who hardly ever left his house and only had visitors at Christmas and Thanksgiving. I remembered thinking how sad and then wishing that same kind of fate on my hateful ass mother.

I lifted the left edge of the old man's welcome mat and sparkling there on the floor like a new piece of expensive jewelry was Tia's extra house key. I hadn't felt that excited since the night I walked into my twenty-fifth birthday party and saw how much my father had done for me. My heart jerked in my chest as I reached down and picked up the lone key quickly. I clutched it in my hand like it was the key to Heaven on judgment day. I looked around again, paranoid that someone might've seen me. Who was I fooling? That damn hallway was empty as hell. I rushed back to Tia's door on shaky legs, but I had the key and that was what was most important. Once I was back at the door I didn't know if I was really ready to be there without Tia. Be brave Ericka. You're not a coward. This is all for Tia. You're not scared. I told myself. I swallowed the hard lump that had formed in my throat as I put the key in the door, turned it and gained access to Tia's apartment.

As soon as I stepped in I felt sick. The key dropped from my hand and I almost dropped down with it. "Oh Tia...where are you?" I began to cry. Being up close and personal with her things made the void of her absence seem much more pronounced than it had been when I was just hearing that she was missing. Standing there now, the reality and gravity of the situation settled into my mind. My girl was missing. Poof! Gone without a trace. My father had said Tia came home after my party, but as I moved slowly around her place, I had the feeling that that was not true. I could still see signs of Tia's party preparation strewn about her apartment. I could smell Tia's signature scent Gucci Guilty in the air too. Tia had been wearing that scent since the designer had dropped it and even before it came to the United States, Tia's father had had the exclusive premiere bottle of the high priced perfume flown in from Paris—the perfume mecca of the world. I would never be able to smell that scent again without thinking of Tia. I walked into her lavishly decorated living room. Tia had always had a flare of flamboyance so the fuscia, bright aqua blue, and black furniture wouldn't surprise anyone who knew her as well as I did. Tia had all glass side tables, furry sitting chairs that were shaped like shoes and her couch was an ultra modern black leather three seater with Swarovski crystal buttons on the backs of it. Even Tia's throw pillows screamed spoiled little rich girl—they were made of hand tuft suede and lace and each one had her name embroidered on them. I noticed that Tia's iPad was still propped up on the little glass top bar that sat a few feet away from her huge, glass terrace doors. I picked up the iPad but it had already run out of battery life so I wouldn't be able to get any clues from there. I turned around and faced Tia's gourmet kitchen. Her kitchen was pristine as usual. Trust me no pots or plates had ever seen the light of day in that kitchen. Tia had told me that when her father bought the apartment for her they had to rip out the entire kitchen and rebuild a new one to her liking. She had a Viking stove and Subzero refrigerator, but she had never used them. Talk about spoiled. I walked through the kitchen and as I was about to exit into the hallway that led to her bedroom, I noticed in the garbage was at least ten little plastic baggies. While I was sure the police had probably come through there, they certainly hadn't messed the place up like I always see them do on T.V. cop shows when they searched a home, but they also had obviously missed some important clues. I bent down and dug into the small trashcan that sat by Tia's sink. I retrieved the baggies and I could tell from the residue they had all contained the same arctic ice shit that Tia had given me that night. With the number of baggies that was there I couldn't be sure if Tia had been just taking the drugs or damn selling them. I slipped one into the pocket of my jacket. I was going to prove to the police and the Cassidy's that this drug shit had come from Tia and not from me. With a big, deep breath, I wrapped my arms around my body to keep it from trembling as I made my way down the slender apartment hallway. Tia's face in all different types of portraits and photographs painted both sides of the hallway walls. She really was a beautiful girl. Some of the pictures on the walls were definitely worthy of Elle and Vogue magazine covers. I cupped my hand over my mouth because it was becoming harder and harder to keep my composure. Memories kept flooding my head. The last time I had walked that hallway, which I always called Tia's walls of fame, Tia had been in front of me giggling about something as usual and she had tripped over her own feet. I was walking so close to her, I had fallen down right on top of her. We had died laughing as we both kept trying to get up. That was right after I had broken up with Cyrus and Tia had called me over for some girl talk and drinks. She always managed to know what I needed at the perfect times.

Now that I think back, Tia was probably high on drugs and I didn't even know it. I hiccupped the sobs that were getting caught in my throat. I had made it to Tia's bedroom door, another place in her apartment that held so many of our friendship memories. The tears fell from my eyes as soon as I walked into Tia's bedroom. It was all typical Tia. Of course her bed wasn't made up. Tia was the type of chick that was used to a maid so that didn't surprise me. There were piles of clothes everywhere. That was also typical Tia. It would take her hours to get dressed just to go to do something as simple as a nail appointment. Tia was very big on making sure her appearances were kept up. I guess she had gotten that vain attitude from her bitch of a mother. I stepped a little bit further into the room and suddenly I had a picture of Tia sitting Indian-style on her bed telling me to come over and gossip about bitches in our school. It was what we did best when we got together.

I looked around some more. I had to crack a small smile when I saw at least fifteen pairs of Giuseppe Zanotti and Christian Louboutin shoes scattered all over Tia's bedroom floor. Those shoes were probably worth over ten thousand dollars in total. Tia didn't play when it came to her designer shoes, handbags and clothes. My girl was sharp. I could just picture her trying on pair after pair of shoes trying to find the perfect ones for my party. Typical Tia. I smiled.

I kicked through the shoes and looked up at the aqua blue pin board that hung over Tia's nightstand. The board was covered with nothing but pictures of Tia and me. I think it spanned all of the age groups we had shared together. I felt instantly sad as I scanned all of the pictures of us. I had a dreadful thought fill my head that maybe those memories were all I would have left of our friendship. I immediately wondered if Tia and I would ever make those types of fun memories again. I plopped down on her bed and inhaled deeply. I opened Tia's nightstand drawer and inside was a bunch of condoms, more drug baggies and what looked like a telephone address book. I pilfered through the junk in the drawer and picked up the black book thinking maybe it had an address or held some phone number or clue as to where Tia might be. I squinted and began thumbing through the pages, propelled by curiosity. After scanning a few of the pages, I could tell that the book was some sort of journal. That kind of shocked me. As long as I had been a friend to Tia, I had never known her to keep a diary or a journal. Tia had always scoffed at me keeping a diary. She would say "writing down everything that happened for the day only lets nosey people into your life when they don't deserve it and preserves memories of shit you might of otherwise wanted to forget." After Tia had told me that I thought about it and I stopped journaling and keeping any kind of diary. Now, I see that she wasn't practicing what she preached at all. This was starting to be a trend with Tia.

I opened up what I now knew to be Tia's journal, to the last page Tia had written. It hadn't been hard for me to find the last page because a little, red, satin ribbon was stuck between the pages to hold her place. I took a few seconds before I started reading and said a silent prayer that God would allow me to be able to handle whatever it was I was about to find out about my best friend, whether it was good or bad.

I began reading the first page. Heat immediately began to rise from my chest, climbing up my neck and finally settling on my cheeks. It was the heat of anger that first grabbed hold of me. But, the more I read, the more my anger began to turn into pure despair and the weaker my legs became. I could feel my mouth hanging open but I couldn't speak. This was all too much for one day. My heart raced painfully in my chest and suddenly my throat felt like someone had their hands around my neck choking me. I dropped the book on the floor. I couldn't read anymore. I couldn't even remain in Tia's house any longer.

"Why Tia? Why? Was anything you ever told me, true? Was everything, even our friendship all based on your lies?" I cried out loud as if in some magical way Tia would be able to hear me. It was a harsh reality but it was definitely starting to settle in with me that I might not really know this girl I thought was my best friend in the entire world.

I raced out of Tia's bedroom and down her hallway towards her front door. There was so much about my best friend that I could've never imagined. I was starting to question everything about our entire friendship. I stumbled for the door trying to be careful not to knock down any of Tia's "wall of fame" pictures, but it was hard because I was so weak I needed to hold onto the walls for support. I was in an even more desperate race to find Tia now, I just didn't know if it was for the same reason anymore. Was it because I was worried about her? Or was it because I wanted to step to her and confront her about all of the lies she had been telling? Either way, I would need to find out what happened to her. Questions definitely needed to be answered, but I realized in order to ever have my questions answered; I was going to have to find Tia first. I rushed out of Tia's building with Preston's eyes on me.

"I thought you came to get some of her things?" Preston asked me. I had forgotten all about the story I had told him. I shot him a look that was so deadly that if looks could kill he would've surely crumpled to the ground.

"Don't fucking say another word to me Preston, just call me a cab right now. And, for the record, if you tell anyone that I was here I will make sure they know that you are sleeping with several male residents of this building and in that case you won't have this little job for long," I hissed, squinting my eyes into evil dashes. Preston looked like he was about to come back with something smart to say, but he thought better of it and quickly snapped his mouth shut. He picked up the phone and called me a taxi right way.

"Oh and one more thing, that little sex change operation you're working on and had Tia stealing hormones from her father for, I knew about that too. I think possession of illegal drugs carries a stiff sentence too," I said viciously before I stormed out of the building and hopped into my taxi. I was feeling both deadly and evil at the same damn time. I was also on a mission to find Tia Cassidy, but not before I made a stop.

CHAPTER 7

Where There's Smoke There's Fire

The entire ride to my father's office building I felt like I had to take a shit, throw up, sneeze and cough. It was my nerves and my temper all rolled into one that was working me over that way.

My stomach was doing somersaults, literally. And my body was so tensed it felt like I was coming down with the flu. I guess that was what stress could do to you.

"Fucking liars. Everyone around me is a fucking liar," I grumbled out loud to myself.

"Is everything ok?" the taxi driver asked me in his thick Middle Eastern accent. I shot him such a glaring, deadly look that he just averted his little beady eyes back to the road and shut his mouth.

"You wait…you fucking wait," I hissed. I kept seeing Tia's journal entries over and over in my mind and for some reason I wasn't really mad at her. It was my father that I wanted to jump on and gouge his eyes out. He was the one that should've known better. How disgusting was he? And now, what did he really know? The more I sat and thought, the worse I felt about the situation. There was no telling how I was going to react when I was finally in front of my father.

My fists were curled tightly and my toes were bunched up in my shoes as the taxi rounded the corner of the block where my father's office stood. The closer I got to confronting him the harder my heart drummed against my chest bones. Taking a deep breath, meditation and even a tranquilizer would probably not have calmed me down at that moment. There was definitely a raging wild fire going on in my brain. I couldn't describe the different thoughts and feelings coursing through my mind at that moment. I guess ringing loud and clear for me was the word betrayal. I hated to think that all of my life I never really knew the real person my father was. The thought both infuriated and scared the shit out of me at the same time. He was really the only person I had in the entire world. So if that got fucked up and was all based on him lying to me, then where would I be? I had a few options in this situation, but letting this shit go without confronting it wasn't one of them. I had to know why. I had to know what had possessed him. I am his daughter! She is my best friend! For crying out loud!

I swear I was jumping out of that taxi before the driver could even fully come to a stop. I threw the cash over the seat and didn't wait for my change. It was late by then and dark outside, but something told me that my father would still be at his office. He often worked late and I knew by the fact that Olla hadn't blown up her cell phone that I had taken from her, that my father must've still been working and hadn't discovered that I had gotten out of the condo yet.

"You better fucking be here Mr. Eric Kane you fucking fake. Your daughter is not the one for the games and I want answers," I mumbled through clenched teeth. I punched in the code to the set of outside glass doors and stormed inside to the second set of heavy wooden doors. I knew those wouldn't be locked since the outside doors were already locked. My father was predictable in a lot of ways, which is why I don't understand how I didn't see the signs. Stupid ass me was just walking around in the dark while everyone else was laughing behind my fucking back.

I was stomping down the carpeted hallway that much I did know, but I was definitely on cruise control. My legs were pretty much carrying me along because my brain certainly wasn't thinking straight. I guess it was a good thing that my muscle memory knew that office like the back of my hand because as angry as I was, I might've walked right into a damn wall had I not known automatically where to go.

ERICKA *Kane*

I had finally made it to the suite where my father's office sat but before I could storm into his river view office space and jump on his ass, I heard a lot of voices coming from the direction of his suite. The voices were kind of elevated, not the usually hushed murmurs of a business meeting. All I know is that the sounds were different enough that they caught me off guard and caught my attention at the same time. For a minute, I was sidetracked from what I had come there to do. It just didn't sound like normal businessmen banter and before I exposed myself, I wanted to know why the conversation sounded so heated.

I flattened my body against the wall opposite the huge window to my father's office and I peeked around. The blinds on the window were half drawn so I could see that my father was practically surrounded by men in black suits. Something about the scene didn't sit right with me. My father was also wearing a suit, but why was everyone standing around like that. Then I saw my father move to his desk and the other men take their seats. My shoulders slumped a little bit. Just a regular old business meeting, I said to myself. Now I would have to wait until he was finished because I wanted my father to have his full focus to be on me when I said what I had to say to him. I bit down into my lip until I drew blood as I stood there. After a few minutes of them all being calm, I could hear that one of the men was raising his voice to my father and it sounded like he was telling him off. My ears perked up like a dog's. This wasn't your average business meeting; that was clear to me now. I stepped closer to the crack in the door so I could listen and try to see. I mean, I didn't want anything bad to happen to my father although I was highly fucking pissed off with him. I listened closely as they spoke.

"Eric, we can't believe that you let us down. We have been doing business with you for so long. We have given you so many things and opportunities here in the United States, but it is as if you don't appreciate what we have done for you. Did you remember that you were a poor boy from a poor farming village in Nigeria when we picked you up from the dirt?" one of the men said to my father. That was the first line in a mental warfare game; make your opponent unsure of himself by bringing up something you know he is ashamed of. I remember my father telling me that and now it was being used on him. My father mumbled something but the man who was chastising him wasn't finished.

"There is no excuse for your shortcomings! You were paid for twenty bodies and you came up short. Even by one it makes a difference when you received so much money for each body. Would you cheat the man in the store and pay for one suit but take two or vice versa? I don't think so! Every time you have to produce lately there has been some kind of problem, I don't understand and the powers that be are growing weary of it," the man continued, speaking in a harsh tone that sounded more like a father yelling at his son than two businessmen having an adult discussion. "That is unacceptable when you got paid for twenty bodies! You have to make this right or you will definitely suffer the consequences…or maybe your family will suffer the consequences instead," the man spat. He was getting on my fucking nerves the way he was talking to my father but I couldn't figure out what he was speaking about either. Bodies? Paid for bodies?

"I told you, one of them got very sick so that was no good. I couldn't send that one along like that or everyone would've gotten infected. When you're dealing with other countries you run the risk of spreading all types of diseases. Would you rather me risk one than an entire shipment and what about the clients…you can't sell sick goods to the client and infect the people who buy from us," my father explained. My face immediately folded into a frown. Bodies? Other countries? Risk of disease? It sounded like he was speaking about animals, but I had never known my father to be into importing or exporting animals. My mind raced in a million directions.

"So you send us the American and she has been nothing but trouble. I would rather one that is sick in body than in the mind like her. She screams. She curses. She is constantly in need. She is a fighter, a biter, and an addict!" the man who had been speaking to my father exploded. "She has become a big liability, but what can I do now until I find a replacement!" the man boomed.

Oh shit! The bodies they were speaking about were human bodies!

"It was a last minute call. I had to produce or else I would have to deal with Kesso's wrath and I did that. I kept up my end of the bargain as usual. So you were not really one girl short. Besides, she is a real beauty and I have even broken her in for myself. I did not know she was an addict until that night. You should have let her go cold turkey and she would've been fine! Her beauty alone is worth more than fifty of those foreigners that you have to dress up and prepare for the clientele," my father snapped back. I didn't think I could take much more for the day. That could not have been my father in there speaking about human beings like they were fucking cattle or animals for slaughter.

My legs got so weak that I collapsed onto the floor and hit the door a little bit with my arm. I quickly jumped back to where I had been standing, but I was afraid I might get caught. When I heard the ruffle of suits inside of my father's office I knew they must've been looking at the door to see where the noise had been coming from. I quickly crawled around to the other side of the office window and hid behind the small piece of wall there. I saw my father peek his head out the door, peer up and down the hallway with a strange look on his face and then he went back inside and closed the door. I had heard all I needed to hear, but I was not finished. With all of the things I had learned, I needed some of the drugs that Tia had had the night of my party to ease my mind. I was raging inside.

I didn't get a chance to confront my father about the fact that I had found out that he had been sleeping with my best friend behind my back, but I had heard enough from eavesdropping to know that my father, the seemingly legitimate business man, was into something much more sinister than imports and exports. It sounded to me like he was importing and exporting human beings and from what I could hear he had fucking exported my best friend to these monsters he was working with. Everything happens for a reason. Now, hiding in the shadows of my father's office I came up with a quick plan. I would follow those bastards and see exactly where they had Tia being held.

CHAPTER 8

Getting Caught Up

S tealing one of my father's corporate cars was the easy part once I was able to sneak down to his secretary's desk, but getting out of the parking lot behind the goons that had been meeting with him seemed like it was going to be more difficult than I expected. It was already after midnight when all of the suit and tie wearing ugly goons filed into the parking garage to get into their heavily tinted black SUVs. I waited until they began starting up their engines before I turned on the black Audi A8 I was sitting in, because I didn't want them to hear my engine purring and get suspicious. I didn't see my father with them, which told me he was probably making phone calls to check up on me.

As soon as the last of the three SUVs began pulling out Olla's cell phone rang in my pocket. The vibration from the phone almost sent me to the hospital with a heart attack. I knew it was my father calling or maybe Olla calling to tell me that my father had called the condo. Either way, I wasn't answering his call and I needed to stay away from him for a while until I was fully calm.

I tossed the phone into the empty passenger's seat and drove out behind the SUVs. My father would realize sooner or later that I was gone, but when he did he definitely wouldn't be able to fucking find me. Not until I saved Tia and came back to confront his ass about all of this.

I followed the caravan of black SUVs to the boat docks that were off of the marina behind Georgetown in DC. All of the men seemed to run behind that one guy...the one that had been yelling at my father in the office. I was quickly able to surmise that whoever he was...he was the boss of my father and everyone around. From what I could see he was tall, broad and black. From a distance I could even see that his skin was so dark you could barely see his facial features. I sat in the Audi a few cars away and watched them head towards a big yacht looking boat that was docked at the marina. I knew then that in order to be able to see what they were doing, I was going to have to follow them and get as close to that yacht as possible. It was risky, but it was the only chance I had at finding Tia. At this point, I was certain that the "American" the man had referred to while speaking to my father was definitely Tia. Of course she was a fighter, a screamer and a biter. Tia didn't take any shit off of anyone so I was glad to hear that these human traffickers had met their match when it came to my best friend.

I remember when Tia had a fight in high school with a boy name Alberto because he had pushed me into a table and caused me to hit my head. Tia jumped on Alberto, who was ten times bigger than her by the way, and she had bit his ear so hard she had almost taken a chunk of flesh out of it. Then she had taken two of her fingers and dug them into Alberto's eye sockets until he was screaming so loud like a girl that he had the entire school watching. Alberto was never the same after that because our entire school would refer to him as a wuss. Those are the types of things that Tia did when she was backed into a corner, so with her basically being kidnapped into a human trafficking ring, I could only imagine how wild she has gone. That made me feel good, but it also worried me. I was worried for her safety. How long would these goons that my father was working with continue to put up with Tia's feisty attitude. Her beauty may have been able to buy her a little bit of time, but that wouldn't last so long if her craziness began to outweigh the benefits of her pretty face. I could almost one hundred percent guarantee that they were keeping her drugged up with some strong shit. Once I heard them refer to her as a drug addict, I knew from then that they would be pumping her up with drugs so that she wouldn't be going through withdrawals. I had to save her.

I crept down to the yacht and I could see them on the top deck talking. Suddenly two or three girls that looked very young surrounded the boss. I squinted to see if either of them were Tia. Unfortunately, Tia wasn't there. I could hear them talking but I couldn't understand what they were saying. Then just like that I saw one of the flunkies come over to pull up the anchor that was holding the yacht steady in the water. Shit! They are leaving! My mind raced and just like that without thinking about my own safety or I guess you could say without thinking at all, I slipped my ass onto the bottom level of the yacht. I found a very small closet and got inside. I guess it was to store linens because that shit was tight as all hell. I stayed there for what seemed like an eternity with the door cracked just a sliver so that I could breathe. I just didn't know what I would see next that would take my damn breath away.

When I first heard the sound of whimpering, I thought maybe it was coming from somewhere outside of the room I was in. It sounded like a wounded kitten or some sort of animal crying because it was hungry. When I listened real good it was obvious to me that the sound was coming from some place close to where I was hiding. I peeked through the crack in the closet door and to the far left of the room was a girl. She was the source of the whimpering and judging by the looks of her, I could see why. My eyes went so wide they started tearing up. The girl was sitting with her knees to her chest, bound with duct tape on her wrists, feet, and mouth. She was completely naked except for the thick dog chain around her neck that was connected to a small metal pole that was next to her. Her hair was wild and bushy on her head and when she lifted up her head I was able to see her battered face. She was black and blue and she looked like she had been crying for days. My mouth was hanging open and my heart began racing wildly. I had really walked into danger and I guess it was just registering with me.

A little voice inside my head was screaming at me telling me to go save the girl and try to run for it. I imagined myself setting her free and running with her as fast as we could back to the car. But, then reality set in on me. How would I ever get her free from that chain that bound her to the pole in the boat? What if she was too weak to run and moved too slow? All sorts of things started running through my head and I knew it wouldn't be a good idea to expose myself yet. My nerves were running wild and my skin suddenly became sensitive to the touch. That little cramped closet was driving me crazy at that point. I couldn't stop looking at the poor girl; all bound up like some wild animal. I quickly had a thought about my father and the fact that he might've been responsible for this happening. Finding out he was into the business of selling other human beings had truly broken my heart into a million pieces.

Then, I started thinking about Tia and wondering if she was being held in the same way. That thought alone made me forget about my own risk and I decided I was going to help that girl. I put my hand on the closet door. My palms were sweaty and more sweat dripped down my back. I was about to spring into action, when I heard the sound of voices and footsteps coming in the direction of the bedroom I was in. I quickly ducked as far back into the closet. I felt horrible that I couldn't help the girl. I could still see her a little bit through the small crack in the door though. Now I couldn't get Tia off my mind at all. Between the fatigue of being out all day and the worry I was feeling, my mind was starting to slip. Shit was getting serious with each passing hour.

Within seconds I saw the two young girls I had seen with the men outside. The girls sauntered into the room like they were two runway models. They giggled and held onto one another. Something about their laughter reminded me of Tia, and myself but it also reminded me of how Tia sounded when she was high. I wouldn't doubt that those two girls were both high on some shit those men probably made them take. As I watched them, suddenly my vision was blocked and that scary man was there. I shrunk back a little in the closet, not wanting to risk him seeing me watching. I could only imagine what he would've done to me if he caught me there. Even identifying myself as my father's daughter probably wouldn't have helped me if that monster knew I was watching him.

I watched the man with the girls gathered around him and I instantly felt a swirl of emotions. Anger was one of the emotions that stood out in my heart. I even felt disgusted and scared that Tia was probably going through a massive amount of torture. One of the young girls was helping the man remove his jacket while the other one took off his shoes. They looked like slaves in the literal sense. I could feel the anger rising from my feet and up to my chest. I could feel my face flushing with anger. All of them, the man and his two slaves, were all acting like they didn't see the bound up girl in the corner. The poor girl had stopped whimpering. I guess she knew that if she kept crying they would do something else to her. I shook my head and crinkled my eyebrows in confusion. What type of animals were these people? A human being bound and gagged and beaten didn't evoke any emotion in any of them, yet I was screaming inside and dying to help her.

Once the man was undressed, he eased back on the huge bed with an evil scowl on his face. One of the girls lit a blunt and gave it to him. The man took a long drag on the blunt and then he pointed in the direction of the captive girl. He didn't even have to say anything to the other two, who looked like his servants. It was like he could just point or snap his fingers and they started doing whatever he wanted. The two girls rushed over to the bound up girl and surrounded her like hungry dogs about to eat a steak. The bound girl lowered her head and hid her face like she already knew what was coming next. Obviously whatever they were about to do was nothing new to her.

"Get up bitch!" the lighter skinned of the two girls screamed. "It's time for you to prove yourself today. No more games, no more bullshit. Kesso is ready for you and you better act right this time. He will not have so much mercy on you as he did before," the light skinned girl hissed. Then she grabbed a handful of the tied up girl's hair while the other girl, a darker skinned girl, cut the tape from her feet. "What you got last time will only be a small version of what you get this time. If you don't act right, we get blamed so I would suggest you get it fucking right," the darker skinned girl growled. Then she lifted her foot and landed a kick in the bound girl's ribs.

"What is your name now?" the light skinned girl asked as she raked the tied up girl's hair roughly. The tied up girl whimpered in pain, trying to reach up and grab the light skinned girl's hand. I couldn't see the abused girl's entire face because the crack in the door was too small, but I could tell she was crying again. The light skinned girl asked the tied up girl her name again, but this time she ripped the duct tape from the girl's mouth with no mercy. The captive girl just cried. "My name is Alicia and I live in Maryland. I don't belong here and all I want to do is go back home," the girl pleaded through sobs. The light skinned girl wrenched Alicia's hair until she fell back down on the floor. The dark skinned girl punched her in the head and kicked her in the ribs again.

"Ahhh!" Alicia screamed out in pain.

"You stupid bitch!" the dark skinned girl spat. "Your name is not Alicia anymore! He told you that your name is Tender and you are from Miami if anyone asks you. You never lived in Maryland and you don't have any family...dumb bitch, do you understand English!" the dark skinned girl gritted as she continued to rain down punches and kicks on the poor girl. My toes balled up in my shoes and my fists curled. I wanted to bust out of that closet so badly and pummel those two smug bitches. I knew that was the man's plan...turning the girls against one another would ensure their loyalty to him. It was the same concept white slave masters used back in the slavery days in the antebellum South. I was seething inside watching this whole thing go down.

"Ten days and you still won't get with the program? You could've saved yourself all of this pain from day one. But no, you want to be a tough girl. Well until you call yourself Tender and say that you're from Miami you will continue to get it. Now…let's go," the light skinned girl demanded, pulling on the girl like she was a pet on a leash.

"My name is Alicia," the captive girl whispered through her battered lips.

"Oh yeah, well he is going to keep raping you until you call yourself the name he has chosen for you. Just do what he says and save yourself. You'll never get out of here so you might as well just give in. We all had to go through the same thing…all of the girls do, but the difference is some of us learn to live with it and be happy and receive the benefits and others end up dead because they didn't comply. One thing is for sure…you won't be going back home either way…dead or alive you will be here forever so make your choice," the light skinned girl growled at the captive girl. Her voice droned on like she had totally given up on her own life. It was like she was repeating words she had rehearsed a thousand times. She was like the man's robot now, doing his dirty work. Both of them seemed brainwashed, like they were going through the motions but weren't really themselves. I forgot what the name of the syndrome was where kidnap victims started believing their captors really cared about them, but I could tell that these two girls were suffering from it. Either that or those two bitches were just pure evil and liked what they were doing.

"Now get over there! You're bringing all of this on yourself!" the light skinned girl barked, making a good show of it for her boss. She shoved the tied up girl towards the bed where the man, who they had called Kesso, was waiting. He sat up with his nasty black naked body exposed. I squinted and thought I could see what appeared to be healed slashes on his chest like he'd been whipped or cut in the past. He rubbed his hands together and licked his huge lips. Then with an evil grin on his face he grabbed the poor girl down towards his naked body. His face was in my direct line of sight now. That was when I could see how ugly he was. The type of ugly where you would compare him as a human to the ugliest animal you'd ever seen. His lips were huge and his nose was flat with just two huge holes like a Gorilla's face.

"Please don't. Please don't." Alicia was pleading now. Kesso laughed then he grabbed her hair and forced her face into his crotch.

"Open your mouth," he said. I could hear his Nigerian accent clearly now. It made my skin crawl too. "Open your mouth and suck it or you know what you get."

"Please!" Alicia screamed out. Kesso punched her across the face so hard spit and blood shot out of her mouth.

"I am sick of your disobedience. You are so lucky that they say you are supposed to have such a tight pussy and will make me good money or else I would've killed you and thrown you over the boat myself," Kesso barked at her. "Now open your fucking nasty mouth!" he hissed. Alicia still tried to fight but it was useless. The light skinned girl came over, squeezed Alicia's cheeks forcefully until she opened her lips and then Kesso forced his dick into her mouth. She was gagging and choking, but he continued to thrust himself as far as he could into her throat. He was panting and huffing like some sort of animal in heat. I hated him more and more by the minute. I just still couldn't fathom that my father would've ever associated himself with people like this. All of the years that my father had been so gentle with me. Taking care of me when my mother abandoned us. My father was the ideal man in my eyes, so to find out now that he had a hand in something like what I was witnessing at that moment surely broke my heart into a million little pieces. I couldn't even think about how I'd ever face my father again, much less confront him about what I had learned about his business dealings. I shook my head left to right trying to keep those invasive thoughts away. I needed to be alert and not daydreaming.

After about ten minutes of Kesso raping Alicia's mouth, he pulled out and splashed his cum all over her face. She was gagging and coughing. Even I wanted to throw up and I wasn't even the one with his nasty body fluids all over my face. I wished at that moment

I had a gun. I would've busted out of that fucking closet and spilled that nasty nigga's brains all over that room. Those two other bitches he has with him would've definitely been toast as well.

"Get up on the bed," Kesso demanded, grabbing a handful of Alicia's hair and yanking on it. Alicia was shaking all over, but she did what she was told. Once on the bed, the other two girls moved onto the bed too. Alicia's was moving her head from side to side frantically.

"Please. What are you going to do to me? Please...please," Alicia pleaded. Kesso slapped her in the face again.

"Shut the fuck up! I want to hear you say your name!" he barked at her.

"Um.....Alici..." she started, but he slapped the words right back down her throat.

"Your name is Tender! Say it! Say the name I gave you!" Kesso hissed, slapping the girl again. My insides were on fire like someone was setting off firecrackers inside my chest.

"What is your name?" he asked again. Alicia's lip was split I could see that from where I was in the closet. Just say Tender. Just tell them your name is Tender so they'll stop. I was saying in my head as if she could somehow telepathically hear me. It was no use. I think Alicia had given up on life and she wanted them to just kill her. No matter what they did she wasn't going to tell them what they wanted to hear. I guess Alicia was thinking that she'd rather die on her feet than live on her knees. I admired her for that. I know most of the girls they brought there had probably given in the very first time they were confronted by Kesso. Not this girl, she wasn't going to let them win no matter what they tried.

"Tie her down," Kesso growled.

"No please! No!" Alicia begged, writhing and trying to get away. It was too late. The two servant girls used arm shackles and leg irons to chain her to the bed. Then, the light skinned girl stuffed a wadded up handkerchief into Alicia's mouth and taped it down.

"You should've just said that your name was Tender. You should've just gotten with the program...now...there's no hope for you," the light skinned girl said.

"Now...bring me what I need," Kesso commanded, an evil sinister grin painting his ugly face. The dark skinned girl jumped off the bed, went to a far corner of the room and brought back a black briefcase. She put it down on the end of the bed and opened it.

"Mmmmm!! MMMM!!!" Alicia began trying to scream through the mouth gag, but her screams only came out as muffled moans and groans. The sound made the hairs on the back of my neck stand up. My lips were trembling and I could not control it. I heard the locks to the black case being popped open. I couldn't see at first what was inside of the briefcase, but after a few minutes, I saw Kesso with what appeared to be a torch. I swallowed hard and I felt like I had a huge lump in the bottom of my stomach. Kesso snapped his fingers at the girls. That's when I saw it. The light skinned girl handed him a branding iron like the ones used on cattle. My eyes grew wide and I clasped my hand over my mouth, just imagining what he was going to do to her. I saw the blue and orange flames spark at the end of the blowtorch, then the dark skinned girl heated up the branding iron while she wore a cruel smirk on her ugly face. I snapped my eyes shut. I couldn't watch them burn that poor girl's skin like she was a damn animal. I kept my eyes closed until I heard the sounds.

"MMMMMMMMMM" I heard Alicia trying to scream. She tried to buck her body in protest but she was no match for the three evil devils that were surrounding her. I could actually hear her skin sizzling like it was cooking in a frying pan. When her moans stopped I just assumed that the poor girl was dead. I slid down to the floor inside of the closet and the tears began flowing from my eyes. All I could do was wonder if the same thing had already happened to Tia. My brain was completely exhausted at that point and I had no idea what my own future held, much less Tia's.

CHAPTER 9

Still In Harms Way

I didn't even realize that I had fallen asleep on the floor of the closet inside of the yacht. It was like the darkness of what I had witnessed, the information I had received about my own father and the danger I knew I was in had all come crashing down on me like a ton of bricks. I had slipped into an exhausted sleep and didn't even realize that someone could've found me hiding and killed me. The risks I had been taking just got more and more dangerous for me by the minute.

I jumped up when I realized I didn't hear anyone in the room anymore. Alicia's screams and moans were gone. The two girls with their taunts and abuse were gone. Most importantly, the evil man who controlled all of them was absent from the room. I was alone again and contemplating my next move.

I got to my feet and peeked out of the closet. The room wasn't just empty, it looked like no one had ever been there to begin with. The bed was made up and there wasn't one thing out of place. There were no chains on the floor, tape or anything that could be used to torture someone apparent around the room. I even had a quick fleeting thought that maybe I had imagined the entire thing from the night before. You would've never known that a young girl had just been tortured there if you hadn't stood there and actually witnessed it with your own eyes. I couldn't tell what time of the day it was because the room was down in the bottom of the boat where the windows were either very small or none at all. I could only assume it was sometime well into the next day because I had been gone a long time and I had fallen asleep there. A quick thought of my father popped into my mind and what he must've been doing at that moment. He was probably going crazy by now looking for me. It wouldn't surprise me to know that he had called the entire police department in five counties looking for me. I didn't miss him one bit because, honestly, I still didn't know what would happen when I finally got the chance to confront him.

It was better for him and me that I didn't confront him right now because the things he had done thus far were really unforgiveable. Sleeping with Tia was low down and dirty enough in my book, but this...selling young girls into slavery to make money and kidnapping girls to subject them to severe abuse...was more than I could've ever imagined my father would do. I was afraid of the karma that would come back on my father for these sins. I just hoped I wasn't in the direct line of what he got as payback.

I shook my head left to right, trying to get those thoughts out of my head. Thinking about my father right now would only make me too weak minded to carry out the mission I had at hand. You can't get weak now Ericka. Stay on track. I gave myself a quick pep talk. I felt slightly better and then it was time for me to make a move.

I slowly eased the closet door open and looked left and right with wide eyes. I didn't see anyone or hear anything so I crept out on my tiptoes. I went to the room door and pulled it back carefully and as quietly as possible. It still made more noise than I would have liked, which made my nerves stand on edge like crazy. Once the door was opened and I was able to peek out, I could see the steps that led up out of the boat. I couldn't tell if anyone might be up on the deck waiting for a stowaway like me. The men I had seen had all been carrying big guns, ugly scowls on their faces and an apparent thirst to kill. I don't even think identifying myself as Eric Kane's daughter would've helped me out if they had found me hiding in the bottom of that boat. I know I was crazy for all of this but I couldn't think about that now. I was already too deep into it to turn back now. With my heart racing, I made a run for the boat steps, but I was very careful coming up out of the opening that led outside. I stopped and listened for a few seconds to make sure those men weren't swarming, but I didn't hear anyone outside. I carefully climbed up the steps being sure to listen closely for voices. Once I got to the top, I shielded my eyes from the bright sunlight. I stayed as low as I could, squinted and looked around to see if I saw Alicia, the two girls from the night before, Kesso or any of his men. I felt a slight air of relief wash over me. There wasn't a soul left on the boat, which was perfect for me. The surroundings outside were totally different too, which meant my father's corporate car was nowhere near where I was at that moment. Which also meant that if I had to run I would have no quick escape vehicle or route. Where I was now was not the same location where I had gotten on the boat. I could definitely tell we were no longer in DC near the docks. The yacht was now parked amongst a bunch of huge cargo ships that looked like they shipped things overseas. In the distance I could see a Carnival cruise ship docked as well. That was when it struck me that this place wasn't as strange as I had first suspected, in fact, something seemed very familiar about it all. I was standing in Baltimore at the port where the overseas shipments came through and the cruise ships docked. I had been down there many times with my father when he was making so-called business runs. Now, shit was starting to become clear for me. My father had been shipping and receiving human beings as cargo all along. He had even taken me down there a few times when he needed to meet with people he called his business partners and associates. How could I have ever known they were all criminals involved in such a disgusting and vile industry as the sale of human beings for a profit? My stomach growled and flipped—a mixture of hunger and the sickness of knowing my father was such a criminal after I looked up to him so much. I couldn't even stand to envision his face in my minds eye right now. I must've been there daydreaming for longer than I had originally intended because I was jolted when I suddenly heard men's voices coming from my left. My heart thumped and a chill shot down my spine. My body instinctively moved into a defensive posture and I ducked down as quickly as I could. Sweat had broken out on my forehead and was running down my back. Peeking over the side of the yacht, I could see some of Kesso's men opening a large cargo crate. The scene was pretty chaotic. The men were yelling something at each other in their language and waving their hands frantically, but nothing would've prepared me for what I saw next. When one of the men stepped aside I was able to see that he was pointing a long, black rifle looking gun towards the opening of the cargo crate. I crumpled my eyes in confusion. Is he going to shoot something that is coming out of the crate? An animal? I started speculating in my mind.

"Let's go! Fast!" that same man screamed in English, his accent still thick. Then he said the same thing in what sounded like two other languages. My eyes widened to capacity and my lips opened slightly without me even telling them to, as I watched a line of girls come trailing out of the cargo crate one by one with their hands on their heads and fear written all over their faces. The men held guns on the line of girls and were constantly shouting things at them and pushing them forward. I couldn't believe my fucking eyes at what I was seeing. It was like something out of a damn movie. There were girls of all shapes, sizes and skin colors in that line. As each one passed I had quick fleeting thoughts about what their backgrounds might've been before they were snatched into this. Some of those poor girls looked younger than fifteen and others looked older than twenty-one. One girl I noticed was even pregnant. The one thing all of the girls had in common was the fear that danced in their eyes. It was so noticeable I could recognize it even at a distance. The girls were dirty, dressed in shabby clothes, looked tired, and some of them were crying. One girl stopped, leaned over and threw up. I am assuming she was sick from whatever long ride they had taken or maybe from something the captors had given her. I could only imagine what it could be. One of the men grabbed her by the hair forcefully, pointed the gun in her face and screamed at her to stand up. She cried out and more vomit came out of her mouth. The man that had been holding her slapped her so hard she fell face first into the dirt. I could see him screaming again, this time he rested the tip of his gun on her back. The girl was clearly struggling to get back on her feet but the gunman did not care. He screamed and waved his gun at her until she was finally able to stand up.

I crept down from the boat and ran behind the cargo crates so that I could get a better look or try to see if maybe I could find Tia amongst those strange girls. I also needed to know where they were taking those girls, because wherever they were going, I had a strong gut feeling that Tia would be there too. This was obviously a well-run human trafficking operation that seemed like it had been going on for years. Everything moved like a well-oiled machine, even the girls in the line being herded like cattle. I guess when my father and the men were speaking in his office about shipments and receiving the goods, they were referring to girls just like the ones I was seeing now.

"Split them up!" I heard one of the men yell. He was holding what appeared to be a very big gun too. "We have to inspect them. Sick ones die if they don't look good enough to keep. We need to fill up all of the vans and if we are short we will have to go out and find replacements before the sales," he followed up. It was like they were speaking about animals and not other human beings. I was appalled to say the least. Who could do some shit like this to another human being? It was all in the name of money. Only sick motherfuckers like my father could just sit by and benefit from other people's pain. I shook my head in disgust and curled my hands into fists. I wanted to kill those men and free those girls, but most of all I wanted to kill my own father. I could only imagine just how much input he'd had in this newest shipment of girls. Not only that, just how much input he had in the fact that these people were probably the ones holding Tia captive somewhere.

I continued to watch as the men went about counting the girls, screaming at them, and inspecting them like they were meat for processing. They were picking and prodding the girls as if picking the best because only the best would make it to slaughter for sale. I think that what I was seeing might've been worse than seeing pigs or chicken prepared for meat processing.

With those bastards screaming in their faces and holding them at gunpoint, the girls were made to open their mouths, turn around, bend over, lift up their shirts, run their hands through their own hair and most demeaning of all was the fact that the men took turns putting their hands down into the girls' pants. Sometimes I could tell those nasty motherfuckers were digging in those poor girls' pants way longer than they needed to and getting their sick rocks off by invading these girls in the worst way. I was growing angrier by the minute just watching that shit. I was tapping my foot and didn't even realize it. I know I was thinking if I had a huge gun I would run out there and drop all of those niggas and free all of those girls.

"Move. Let's move them now to the houses. Not a lot of time before the delegation gets into town and there is money to be made. All of them have to be check, prepped and made ready for the selection," one of the men yelled out. He seemed to be one of the team leaders of this whole thing. I remembered seeing him at my father's office. Something about him made me very uncomfortable inside, but it was also something familiar about it.

My heartbeat sped up when I heard that they were taking the girls to be prepared for some sort of sale, but I was happy to hear that there was going to be a place the girls would be transported to. The place the man referred to as the house is probably where I wanted to go to find Tia. I pictured it as one big huge, dirty brothel of women being held against their will. All sorts of shit started running through my mind, but the one thing I didn't think about was the real danger I was putting myself into.

As the men turned around to start loading the girls into vans a pang of panic shot through my stomach and chest. I got desperate, I couldn't just let them leave without knowing where they were going and risk never finding out where Tia might be. In a strictly insane move and with a blank, racing mind, I ran around to the line of girls and I joined the back of the slowly moving line. Yes...yes I did it. I added myself to the bunch of trafficked human slaves all in a desperate attempt to find my best friend.

I know it now that it was the craziest thing I could've ever done in my lifetime, but at the time, I felt like I had no choice. I couldn't help but feel like every single thing that had happened to Tia was my fault. After all, it was my father that had seduced Tia and sold her into this ring. I was going to save my best friend if it was the last thing I did.

We were all being led to a caravan of waiting black vans. I looked ahead to the front of the line from where I stood at the back and I noticed that as each girl climbed in, one of the men used a little metal number counter to click off the count. I guess they were always verifying how many girls they had just in case someone got stupid and tried to escape. Sweat broke out on my forehead and my heart started throttling. I quickly realized that I hadn't been accounted for in the men's original count, which meant, if they found me in the line they would get suspicious. I couldn't afford for them to realize that I wasn't one of the girls who had come over on that cargo ship. As the line moved forward I knew it was only going to be a matter of time before they got to me. I was also dressed much nicer and cleaner than the other girls, which might stick out to these men.

Shit! I have to come up with a distraction...a plan...something. I said in my head. I had to think fast about how I could make sure I wasn't busted being an infiltrator. Sweat started burning underneath my arms and my stomach started rolling as I continued to panic inside. As I stepped closer to the guy with the clicker, I had to think fast. I looked around thinking of how I could get this done. Suddenly an idea popped into my head. I quickly stuck out my foot and kicked the girl in front of me in the back of her legs. I kicked her hard enough to knock her down, but not so hard that it would be readily apparent why she fell in the first place.

"Agh!" the girl screamed as she fell forward. "You bitch you kicked me!" she growled. Her fall caused an almost domino effect as she fell into the girl in front of her. The men ran to the back of the line to see what all of the commotion was. They found two or three girls on the ground and started yelling at them.

"Get up! You trying something funny?! Get up before I spill your brains on the ground! Get up now!" The men were pointing and screaming so much and dragging the girls up off the ground roughly that they were fully distracted and didn't even notice me at all. Yes! Good thinking Ericka! It worked! I told myself, smiling inside but not daring to crack a smile on my face. That was just what I needed, a boost to my confidence and also a welcomed distraction.

I quickly stepped around the commotion and the girls who had fallen without looking suspicious or noticeable. Those dudes didn't even catch a glimpse of me and my clothes or the fact that with my beauty, newly done eyebrows, nails, and gleaming skin that I clearly didn't belong with that group of girls. Even though it had been a long day and night and I was hella tired, I looked one hundred percent better on my worst day than those girls looked all together. I continued behind the other girls in the line and quickly blended myself in. The guy with the counter had been distracted enough for me to climb up into one of the vans without being counted and without looking strange and out of place. I climbed all the way in the back and took a seat in a corner. I put my head down so my face wouldn't really be seen. I breathed a sigh of relief that I had made it into the van, but I was scared as shit at the unknown things to come. Before long two of the men with guns got into the van, speaking roughly in their language. They had walkie-talkies that they used to communicate with the other men in the other vans that had been packed up with girls. I could make out a few of the Nigerian words, but not enough to figure out what they were saying. However, I did hear them say my father's name and my ears perked right up. I lifted my head up and stared up front trying to make out what they were saying about my father. I was practically looking down their throats; that was how hard I was watching, until one of the men glanced into the rearview mirror and caught me. A flash of heat came over me and I quickly averted my eyes back down to my lap. As bad as I wanted to lift my head up and look at him to see if he had become suspicious of me, I was too afraid that he might be staring right back at me. I swallowed the lump that had formed in the back of my throat and fought the urge to look. Instead, I decided to look around at all of the victims that were being held against their own will.

I looked around and studied the faces of the girls in the van and I just wanted to cry. If ever I had felt like a spoiled ungrateful little pampered bitch it was right then. Who was I to ever complain again when I didn't get what I wanted for my birthday or Christmas or everyday for that matter. This was what real oppression looked like, not like the stupid whining and complaining I often did when I didn't get my own way.

All of those girls in that van were raggedy, sad, downtrodden and abused. It was so glaringly apparent that I didn't even have to question it twice. Most of them stunk like high hell, had rings under their eyes and had hair so wild it looked like it had never been touched by a comb, much less a beautician. Some of them had scowls on their faces like they were angry about their situation, but others sat sobbing quietly. One girl had a black eye already, which was probably the result of her trying to fight for her life before being hauled off into slavery. Most of them had bruises some place on their bodies. I could only imagine what they had gone through. All of my life I had lived like a queen. I had been given everything a girl could ask for, but I could tell these girls were probably from some of the poorest places in the world. My father was responsible for this shit! What a fucking piece of shit!

I heard two girls speaking about being sold to these men by their own parents for as little as one hundred dollars. It broke my heart, I could remember getting one hundred dollars as young as six years old and spending it on junk at the mall. I had been living off of money my father made selling these same types of girls into an uncertain life. As the van bumped along and I rubbed elbows with one of the girls sitting next to me, something inside of me was changing. I was growing cold down to my core and I wanted revenge on the people who had done this to these poor innocent lives. I couldn't exactly put a finger on whom I was going to get first once I found Tia, but a lot of motherfuckers were going to either die or suffer when I was done exacting swift moral justice on their asses. During the entire ride to the unknown place that held a fate that I was unsure about, I was plotting the type of revenge that could ruin an entire nation. I was going to get justice for all of these girls. I was going to make sure that if I got out of this shit alive I was going to rise to power and fuck up the whole game.

CHAPTER 10

Infiltrated

The ride was so long and the smell inside of the van was so bad that by the time we pulled up to the house in southern Maryland I had a splitting headache and felt weak in the knees. I had been nodding in and out of sleep and that was probably the only thing that had saved me from throwing up from the odor.

I jumped frantically when I heard banging on the side of the van.

"Let's go! Get them out! Haul them inside! Time is money!" the ringleader of the gunmen was screaming and banging. I guess fear and shock was the best tactic he could come up with to ensure compliance. All of the girls who had fallen asleep jumped up and started looking around wild eyed and scared to death. A few of them were mumbling and a few were crying already. I looked out at the house and it looked like something from a scary movie. It was a non-descript wooden house with a long porch outside. All of the windows were completely covered with shutters and then thick metal bars covering the shutters. A prison. That was the first thing that came to my mind when I took it all in. A fucking, haunted prison was what it looked like there.

There were so many men with guns standing around outside of the house, you would've thought we were really being offloaded at a prison camp or something. There were armed guards in front of the house, at the side of the house and on the porch.

"Out! Out! No funny business or you die!" one of the gun toting men screamed as he waved his gun in our faces. I quickly wondered how tough he would be if he didn't have the fucking machine gun. How tough would any of them be against vans filled with desperate girls ready to fight for our lives? It was no use in dwelling on that idea because the fact still remained those men had big guns that could destroy us on impact.

We loaded out of the vans one by one. We were lined up and again, I became extremely nervous that I would be called out or noticed. The men were discussing our fate when suddenly one of the girls at the opposite end from where I was standing collapsed. It was just like someone had pushed her roughly to the ground the way she fell. It was the same girl that had thrown up and had gotten abused for being sick back at the docks in Baltimore. Two of the men rushed over to her.

"Get up! Stop this shit and get to your feet right now!" one of the men screamed at her.

"I...I...can't," the girl croaked out, lifting one of her hands in surrender. "Make her get up now! We cannot have the boss come out here and find her this way! Get up!" A bunch of the men rushed over to her and surrounded her. They were screaming at her to get up, but she could barely move. She raised her shaky hands to her head and covered her ears. The men continued to scream and get in her face and berate her. I could see her body trembling and her eyes were drawn into slits. She lay there making no more efforts to get up. The girl was clearly sick, but they didn't care. They kept screaming at her. I saw all of the fight going out of her body. It was like she knew before any of us what would happen next but she didn't care. She just had nothing left to give them and it was clear that whatever sickness she had she was not going to make it.

"Get up!!!" the ringleader screamed one last time. His screaming was to no avail. The girl just curled her body into a fetal position and lay there sobbing.

BANG! BANG! Two shots rang out. Moans and groans of sorrow drifted down the line of girls as we all watched blood leaking into the dirt where the girl lay.

I had jumped so hard urine dripped out of my bladder. I threw my hands up over my mouth as I watched the sick girl's brains splatter onto the ground. I was trying my best not to bend over and throw up myself. I could smell the fresh scent of newly spilled blood wafting in the air even though I wasn't right next to the dead girl. Some of the other girls started screaming and crying, they were unable to hold in their pain any longer. The men zeroed in on anyone who was crying and threats were being hurled like rice at a wedding. I was too much in shock to even register that kind of emotion. My eyes were fixated on the blood. There was so much of it. The girl's face, scrawled up into a painful frown was now painted on the insides of my eyes. I had never witnessed death up close in my life before and this wasn't what I had envisioned for my first time. I could feel my entire body vibrating with tremors. My chest was heaving up and down and I could barely move my feet when the men started hollering and herding us forward towards the entrance of that scary looking house. I was regretting this little adventure to find Tia now. How could I be so stupid as to put myself in that type of grave danger? There was no way for me to turn back now, but worse, there was no way for me to know what was to come. These people were clearly more deadly and dangerous than I could have ever imagined and now I was there with no one to protect me. I was there because I had taken myself there, but I had no way of knowing how I would take myself out of there.

The inside of the scary looking house was much nicer than the outside had ever let on that it would be. In fact, I was really shocked to see such a decent interior given the fact that they were herding sex trafficked humans there and the outside resembled a haunted prison camp.

There was a large foyer with nice light colored hardwood floors, nice brown and black leather couches sat around the foyer and in a huge sitting area to the right of the foyer. The furniture looked expensive too. Oddly, just beyond the foyer area there was a counter as if the inside of the house had been fashioned into a business establishment. There was an older black woman sitting behind the counter. She wore huge knotty twists in her hair, no make up and a loose fitting dress that resembled almost a housekeeper's uniform. She stepped from behind the desk with a stack of papers and a clipboard. Business as usual I guess. Never mind the dead girl outside with her brains laying in the dirt. I said to myself as I eyed the woman evilly.

One of Kesso's men walked up to the woman and spoke to her in their language. The two of them shared an inappropriate laugh and then turned towards us girls. The gunman pointed at all of us girls and the woman squinted to get a better look. She wrote something down and then she came out from behind the counter. Her face wasn't kind, but her eyes seemed to signal that she really did feel sorry for us. I figured she was probably putting on a hard face just to mask how she really felt about the situation. I mean what kind of woman wouldn't feel sorry for other women that were being sold as sex slaves and abused in the process?

"I will get them all cleaned up and ready to go. Everyone from all houses will be at the big house tonight because of the arriving delegation. We have to make sure they are fed, cleaned, shaved, dressed and ready to go in a short time. I hate it when you all bring them so late. I like to at least give them all a one on one about the rules and about how they can make this a better situation for themselves," the woman said as she walked up and down the line of girls surveying. It was like she was already picturing in her mind what she would do and how she would dress us up.

"Ah well. I guess Kesso will just have to hope and pray that he has a good bunch here. The last few had some in them that were too much trouble to be worth it," the woman was saying. I locked eyes with her for half a second. She stopped right in front of me and stood face to face with me. She was so close I could smell the Listerine on her breath and the cigarette smoke in her clothes. I quickly looked down at my feet, afraid to hold that uncomfortable eye contact with her.

"This one…she looks too good. Where did she come from?" the lady asked, touching my face like she didn't believe it was real. My heart started beating so fast it felt like it would come up out of my throat. Two of the men rushed over to me and pulled me out of the line at gunpoint. I was shaking so badly I couldn't even feel my own legs. Fear had a tight grip around my throat. I just knew I was about to die.

"She has on designer clothes and her eyes…too healthy. No trauma. No crying. Looks rich to me," the lady said as she circled around me. The men started yelling and pushing me, pointing their guns in my face. I put my hands up to cover my face.

"No! No! I stole these clothes before they grabbed me. I could not be rich…no my father is a poor man from the country," I said, laying on a thick Nigerian accent. The lady looked at me shocked. I know she was expecting me to speak like an American, but I had fucked her whole head up.

"Believe me. I am not rich," I continued, clasping my hands together like I was praying in an attempt to garner their mercy.

"Hmph. I'm going to be watching this one," the lady said signaling them to put me back into the line. I was pushed backwards with the tip of a machine gun.

"Let's go. Time is money. There is much to do with this bunch. They are important because we have a lot of men that want younger ones tonight. From the list that I have there are at least ten that are under eighteen and that will be perfect for those sick ones who like little girls," the lady said.

"All of you! Let's go! Time is money and so are you!" She called out, clapping her hands like we were dogs. Clearly she was a bitch and I had decided right then and there that whenever I got a chance to exact some revenge that bitch would be included on my list.

We were all taken down into a basement area that didn't look like it even belonged as part of that house. I mean, if you had put the outside of the house together with that basement then it would've matched, but the basement didn't look like it was part of the nice upstairs floor of the house.

It was dank, dimly lit, cold and smelled like mildew down there. I couldn't ever remember being in a place so vile in my entire life. In all of our homes I had never had a need to go into any basements or attics.

I looked around the underground pit and shook my head slightly. There were flat, bamboo pallets on the dusty concrete floors and that was it. All of the girls scrambled to find a spot like they already knew what to do in a place like that. I was left standing there, at a lost, searching for a place to sit. Finally, I found a corner and I slid down to the floor. I did not get a chance to get a bamboo pallet so my ass was killing me sitting on that hard concrete. I had no choice. I surveyed the room to see if there were any ground level windows that might be exploited as an escape. No such luck. There were no windows in sight. Just dark gray cinderblock walls that were probably so sound proof that no one would hear us screaming down there even if we tried to stage a revolt.

"They are going to call us one by one," a girl whispered to me. "They are going to do things to us to make sure that we can take it so when we go to the buyers we won't mess things up," she continued. I whipped my head to the left, surprised to hear any of the other girls speak.

"How do you know?" I asked her.

"Because, that's what they did when we got taken. Everything they do is organized and they do it over and over and over," she told me. She started twiddling with her fingers nervously

"Where did you come from?" I asked her, noticing that she didn't have an accent at all.

"I'm from Philly. They snatched me off the street walking the track for my pimp. Really, they tricked me into the car, then I was taken to Baltimore and thrown into that container thing with all of those African girls," she explained. I could feel the rage rising up from my feet and rushing to my head.

"One girl told me it was because a few of the African girls had died on the ride over so they needed to keep their numbers up so they take girls right off the streets," the girl said. "But they kept moving us and counting us and examining us and moving us and counting us. It was crazy."

"What's your name?" I asked her, my voice going low. I really felt like crying based on what she was telling me.

"Aubrey," she whispered. "But don't ever call me by my real name. If I ever get out of this shit, I don't want them to know who I really am."

I had to think long and hard about that. Her words were ringing loudly in my ears. If I ever get out...if I ever get out...if I ever get out. I kept repeating those words to myself. That was the first time it had really dawned on me that getting out of here alive wasn't a promise; instead, it was a very big IF. I had taken so many things for granted in my life, but right there in that basement with all of those girls I promised I wouldn't ever take anything else for granted.

CHAPTER 11

There's Trouble Around Every Corner

Aubrey and I spoke for a while until the guards had come in and started calling girls two and three at a time. I had fallen asleep before they finally called me. One of the men tapped me with the end of his gun and made me get up. I had jumped up, scared as shit. It was no joke being woken up at the end of a big ass gun.

"Lets go! Up! Up!" he barked. I was dazed and confused, my mind cloudy with sleep but within seconds I was on my feet. I was led by gunpoint up the stairs out of the basement. Once I was back in the foyer there were three women, dressed in maid's outfits with their heads tied up in scarves waiting for me. They were with another man who was holding a gun too.

The theme around there was going to be that everything was by force and at gunpoint.

"Come with us," one of the maid women said softly. I looked at her confused, but out of the corner of my eye a man with a gun changed any thoughts I might have had about protesting. I ambled forward still a little out of it.

I was led up a set of big stairs that sat between the foyer and the kitchen inside the house. I followed one of the women up the stairs and the other two trailed behind me.

"This way," the maid woman in front of me said, extending her arm towards a waiting room. I had tried to look down the long hallway once I got to the top of the landing, but I was pushed in the back and yelled at by a man like they didn't want me to see the other doors and other rooms that were up there. Once inside the room that the woman led me to, the man with the gun sat in a chair in one corner with his gun resting next to him like he was used to being in there. He put his feet up on a small table and leaned back in the chair as if that was the first break he had been able to take all day. It was a smug show of arrogance if you asked me. I instantly hated him just as much as I hated Kesso and was starting to hate my father.

"Come," one of the maid women said softly. I was expecting more abuse, but she seemed pretty decent towards me. She handed me a white towel.

"Take off your clothes...everything," she said in a soft, yet demanding tone. "Just cover up with this until they're ready for you." She would not look me in the eyes at all. That is how I knew that she knew everything happening there was wrong on every level. I grabbed the towel from her and bit down into my bottom lip.

I felt tears welling up in my eyes. I wanted to scream out and tell this woman who I really was. I wanted to urge her to help all of the girls there to escape. I wanted to just reach out and shake her shoulders and ask her how she could participate in such a horrible business. A quick glance over at the man with the gun in the corner quickly changed my mind. I slowly began taking off my clothes and finally I lost it. I couldn't stop the tears from falling freely.

"No need to cry. Hurry up and get undressed before they get upset," the woman whispered to me. She took a quick look over at the guard dog, but he had not heard her.

Finally I was out of all of my clothes and standing there trying to cover what I could with my arms and hands. I was shivering although the entire room was warm. A door opened to my right and I jumped. I spun around, eyes wide, body trembling. Two other women that I had never seen before walked in, one was holding what appeared to be a doctor's bag. My eyebrows went low on my forehead, but my eyes were wide looking at them.

"Over here!" a tall, dark skinned woman that looked more like a man screamed at me. She was pointing at the bed. I couldn't move. It was like my feet were rooted to the floor in place. I guess my brain was telling me it was too dangerous so it wouldn't send the signals to my body to move.

"Over here now! Now!" she yelled. I still couldn't bring myself to move. The next thing I felt was the cold steel of the man's gun on the base of my skull. I knew that would eventually happen. He had been waiting for his moment anyway.

"Move now!" the man screamed, then I heard some sort of click. Suddenly my feet were shuffling forward as if someone had flipped an on/off switch inside of my brain. I was thrown down on the bed roughly. I couldn't hold onto that tiny towel the nice lady had given me, so all of my body was exposed now.

"Put your legs up!" the man looking woman shouted.

"Please don't," I whispered. "Please." My thighs were trembling so fiercely you would've thought I was standing outside in zero degree weather.

"Quiet her mouth or I can't work," the man looking woman growled to the other women. The other lady, the nicer one, came over and touched my forehead. For a quick second I thought of the one time I could remember my mother showing me a little bit of affection. Just as quick as that thought came into my head, it disappeared again.

"It will be over soon. It will hurt less if you cooperate," the nice lady said in a soothing tone. I had no idea what the fuck she was talking about until I felt it.

"Agggh!" I screamed as the man looking woman shoved a speculum into my pussy. I had only ever had one GYN exam and I remembered it feeling just as bad as this. "Stop it! Stop it!" I screamed, trying to kick my legs. The man with the gun was back. And this time he rested the tip of the gun on my forehead as I lay there helplessly. I swallowed my screams back down my throat like a handful of hard marbles, but that didn't change the pain shooting through my body as that fucking transvestite looking bitch defiled me in ways I couldn't imagine. She had her face all between my legs and even after she removed the speculum she stuck three of her fingers deep inside of me, pressed on my stomach and moved her fingers around. I had never felt so humiliated in my entire fucking life.

It seemed like hours of torture in that room. I was given a full gynecological exam. My anus was probed. My mouth and teeth were checked. My pussy, armpits, legs and arms were waxed until they were bald and smooth as a baby's ass. My hair was washed and conditioned and styled. Beautiful professional style makeup was applied to my face. My nails and toes were re-done and finally I was given a small salad and some water to drink. I had scarfed down the food like it was the last meal on earth. After I ate, I was dressed in a beautiful lavender Nicole Miller dress, and purple, blue and gold Brian Atwood heels. It was like a professional dress fitting in that room. Those women nipped and tucked and used double-sided tape to keep things in place that they didn't want to see exposed. I couldn't believe the lengths they were going to but I felt like a beauty queen when I was done, except, I was there against my will with no idea what was about to happen next.

"This one is far superior to the rest. She needs to be with the president of the delegation. He always gets the best out the bunch. He likes them young, but I think he will take this one…just beautiful…just beautiful," the woman said to the other. I didn't know what all of that meant but I was sure I would soon find out.

"She is ready to be with the others now. But be careful with her. Something is different about this one and I just can't put my finger on it. I usually have good instincts…this one is beautiful, but might be a handful of trouble," the woman said to the man guarding me.

The man got up from the chair, grabbed my arm and pushed me towards the door. "She better not cause any trouble because I would love to have my way with her and then do away with her," the man said snidely. Then he walked over, grabbed my head forcefully and crushed his mouth on top of mine.

"Mmmm," I moaned in protest trying to push him away. I was no match for his strength and before I knew it he had forced his nasty, smoke stinking tongue between my lips. He let out a maniacal laugh when he let me go.

"Stop it! You will destroy her make up and you will sully her before the delegation gets to pick. You will be reported if you do that again," the nicer woman told the man with her eyes hooded over and her lips pursed. She walked me back over to the vanity so she could fix my makeup and hair. Through the mirror on the vanity I looked at the guard's face very good because I wanted to make sure that when I came back for my revenge, he would be one of the first people to feel the fucking wrath.

Finally I was ready to "be with the others" as the women who'd dressed me had said. I walked slowly out of the door with a feeling of dread dancing in my chest. As beautifully as I was dressed and as glamorous as the clothes I had on were, it didn't change the fact that I had a machine gun pressed into the center of my back.

I was led down the long hallway and as I passed each door, I craned my neck in an attempt to see inside. Some of the doors were opened and I could see girls going through the process I had just gone through. Most of the doors were closed, which left me to only imagine what was happening on the other sides of those doors. As I ambled forward, I was overwhelmed by a feeling that my best friend was somewhere in that house of horrors waiting to be selected just like me. I said a silent prayer that my gut feeling was right and that I would see Tia. As I came upon the second to last door in the hallway I started to feel a little anxious. I wanted to just scream out Tia's name to see if she was there, but that would've just gotten me a beat down or worse, it would've gotten my brains spilled by gunfire like the sick girl.

"Inside!" the man with the gun shouted at me once we had reached the room. I stopped for a few seconds because I was just a little taken aback.

"Inside I said! Inside now! He barked. Then he pushed me through a doorway that led to another large room. I spun around and around once I stepped inside. I was in shock at how many beautifully dressed girls were there. It reminded me of what I would imagine the Ms. America pageant to look like backstage right before the evening gown competition. Every one of those girls were magazine cover worthy.

Some of the girl's faces I recognized from the vans and others I had never seen before. That was a good sign because it gave me hope that if I didn't recognize everyone that meant some girls that were there had been there a long time or were from different houses. I was even more hopeful now that I might run into Tia. Trust me I was scanning that room like a hawk to make sure I didn't miss Tia. It was definitely a eye opening experience being there. There was one thing everyone had in common, we had all been primped and prepped for whatever crazy thing was to come. There were girls dressed in Nicole Miller like me, but some others wore high-end designers like Herve Leger and Diane Von Furstenberg. It was crazy to me that these men would snatch women off the street to be part of the sex trade, but dress them up in clothes the girls probably wouldn't otherwise be able to afford.

"Sit! Everyone sit! Now!" a tall man demanded, raising his hand like a teacher quieting a rowdy class. He didn't have a gun, but there were two men on both sides of him with their guns drawn and at the ready.

All of us women scrambled to find a seat. Personally, my feet were already killing me in those heels so I was glad to have to sit down.

"You all are here for a reason. You can accept that or you can keep trying to fight it. As I understand one of you had to be put out of her misery today. I don't want to see that happen to any more of you. If you try to run you will be hunted, caught and killed. You have nowhere else to go and if you try to leave your families back home will suffer too. This is a very powerful organization and we have a lot of political protections in this country and abroad. Please be good girls and don't make us do anything we will regret later," the man announced, spewing his fear tactic propaganda to all of us. Some of the girls were looking scared and wide-eyed, but I wasn't. Political protections? Fuck you and your political protections. I was seething inside at that man's arrogance. How dare he! I had somewhere to go and I knew better than to think those bullies could do anything to my family. I just hoped I wasn't sadly mistaken to think that my father would accept me back once he found out that I had uncovered his secrets.

When the group of men everyone had been referring to as the delegation arrived at the house there was sheer pandemonium. Some of the girls that had been there longer than me had come with an eagerness to get chosen as a "date." I actually couldn't believe the process and more shocking was the type of men that were in this so-called delegation.

I was the first girl to get selected that night by the group of well-dressed men in suits that had come into the room where all of us girls had been lined up for selection. It was like a real slavery line from four hundred years ago with us standing there letting men touch our breasts, look in our faces, touching our hair and smelling us to see if we were good enough for them. I immediately recognized the Armani suits, Rolex watches, and David Yurman cuff links these men were wearing. This told me right away that these weren't just regular johns off the streets, these were men of privilege and wealth buying women to share their beds and time with. I was disgusted down to my core watching them make their selections. I could smell the liquor emanating from the men and tell by their demeanor that wherever they had come from, they had been partying pretty hard already. I came to the conclusion that this was the very important delegation of foreign nationals I had heard Kesso's men referring to earlier. There were men of all different races in the group, but they all seemed very familiar with one another. It was like they had been looking forward to this part of the night most of all. I guess after whatever business they had taken care of, whatever drinks and dinner they had shared, now they were coming to have a good time and have their sexual needs met. Us captive girls were going to be the center of their good times and that was clear. I could hear them remarking on our beauty or lack thereof and making lewd comments about things they were going to do to us. I was nervous, but for some reason, I didn't have the same fear that I could tell the other girls were experiencing. I wasn't scared at all to be chosen. In fact, I was feeling pretty confident that whomever chose me was going to learn that I was going to be their worst fucking nightmare.

"Her, I want her," a tall, white man with an English accent slurred his words and pointed to me. He reached out and squeezed a handful of my left breast. It took all of my resolve not to slap his hand away and kick him right in the balls. He had a lazy grin on his face and his icy blue eyes seemed evil to me.

"You are beautiful and I only like them like you," the white man garbled, putting his face close to mine. The mixture of alcohol and expensive cigars on his breath made me want to gag. I stood back, hesitant to step towards the man. More like defiant against going with his sloppy drunk ass.

"You...go!" one of the armed men shouted at me waving his gun towards me. I stood there looking dumbfounded at him and at the man who had selected me. It was settling in my brain that I was being sold to a man like a piece of meat.

"Now! You go or you suffer! Move! Now!" the guard boomed in my face, waving his hand menacingly at me. The white man was smiling like a sly fox.

"C'mon...I won't bite you," he said. "Not yet anyway," he followed up, laughing like a maniac.

"One last warning....go!" the guard hissed. One of the women who had been handling all of us came over and gently pushed me in my back. I stumbled forward with my legs shaking and my mind racing in a million directions. The white man grabbed hold of my arm and pulled me into him. He had that stupid lazy grin on his face and his tongue was doing something that made him look crazy. He groped my ass right there in a room full of people. He laughed and whispered something lewd in my ears. The man couldn't keep his hands off of me. There would be no waiting until he had me alone. I could feel his erect manhood pressed into my thigh as he continued his unwanted exploration of my body.

"Why don't we wait until we are alone," I whispered in the sexiest voice I could find under the circumstance.

"Good idea…when I get you alone it will be more than you bargained for," he said. I could tell he was a pervert just waiting to do things to me that he'd probably never dream of doing to his own wife. I had immediately noticed the light spot on his left ring finger. Although the wedding ring was missing, I could tell it had been there probably a few minutes before he'd arrived to buy a girl for the night. Just like my father, a married family man participating in a business that was so disgusting that he ought to burn in hell.

I bit down into my bottom lip to try and keep my cool, but I was raging inside like a wild fire. Something inside of me was telling me to say hell no I'm not going with this white devil piece of shit, but something else inside of me was telling me that I had to play along with this whole thing in order to save Tia and now to save all of the girls there. Yes, that's right. I had decided that it was going to be up to me to break up this little slavery ring and free all of the girls that were being held against their will. I was Ericka Kane and I was going to be the bitch with power that conquered all of these men one day. All of these tough guys walking around hiding behind machine guns weren't going to be a match for me once I was able to get my plan together. I was going to be like their worst nightmare come to life. They didn't know it yet, but they all had met their match in the form of a young, pampered rich girl turned vengeful bitch.

CHAPTER 12

Getting Free

That nasty white motherfucker groped me all the way down the hallway, down the stairs and outside of the house. He was so close to me for the entire time I had almost stumbled down the stairs face first in those heels. He kept saying nasty things to me and licking my neck and the side of my face. I was disgusted down to the core of my soul. Several times I was tempted to slap the shit out of him, but I decided I would save my anger and let it well up inside of me. Anger had always given me courage as a kid and it wasn't going to be any different now.

Once we were finally downstairs and outside, I was put into a black Lincoln Town car with the white, devil pervert. Inside the car the devil who had purchased me was practically sitting on top of me before I could fully settle into the back seat. He was too busy moving his hands all over my body to even communicate our destination to the hired driver.

The driver must have already known where we were going because the man didn't say anything to him and the driver just pulled out and began driving. I pushed the man off of me and looked at him with a scowl.

"Why don't you tell me your name or something? You're touching me, but don't you want to get to know me?" I asked in a disgusted tone. I could see a light bulb going off in the man's eyes. It was like he hadn't even thought about the possibility of communicating with me since he had paid for me.

"I'm Serge," he said looking at me seriously for a long minute.

"I'm Tender," I lied, coming up with something as quickly as I could. I had been thinking about Alicia a lot so I called myself the name they had been forcing her to take.

"Good Tender. I hope your insides are as tender as your outside. I paid a lot to be with you tonight and I expect to get all of my money's worth. Can you do that? Give me my money's worth?" Serge huffed into my ear, as he wasted no time going back to putting his hands up my dress.

My nostrils were flaring and I clamped my legs together on his hand. He jumped up so he could look at me. His face was crumpled into an evil snarl and his icy blue eyes were glinting with hints of malice.

"Listen slave girl, I will report you if you play any games. They will come and get you and I will make sure they don't have any mercy on you. I will touch you, fuck you, lick you and do whatever I want to you for twenty four hours…that is what I paid for and I intend to get every dollars worth," Serge growled as he roughly clamped down on my thigh. I winced from the pain of his abuse, but I kept my cool too.

"Now open your fucking legs and let me test out what I bought," he grumbled, moving his hand back to the opening between my legs. I tried my best to relax. I closed my eyes, eased the muscles in my legs and allowed him to thrust his hands up into my crotch. I murmured my disapproval and I turned my head to the side so he wouldn't see the tears rimming my eyes. I wasn't going to give him the satisfaction of knowing he was dominating me. That's what men like Serge paid for…the fantasy of domination and abuse. It was all because they probably had no power at home or at work or in their lives in general. Abusing helpless girls was the only thing that made them feel like real men.

Serge fingered my pussy, licked my neck and fondled my breasts for the entire ride. I was dying inside, but I wanted to find my friend so I played along.

"We are here sir," the driver finally announced. His words couldn't have come any sooner for me. Serge finally came up for air and looked around. He smiled wide and rubbed his hands together like he was about to make some deadly scientific concoction. I looked out of the window frantically looking for landmarks that I could file away in my memory for use later. I was shocked to see that we had pulled up in front of the doors of a huge, beautiful mansion. There were manicured lawns with those expensive shrubs that all of the rich people in my neighborhood had in front of their homes. There was a circular driveway with several luxury cars and other Lincoln Town cars parked there. The columns on the marble porch leading to the front door of the mansion gave the home an iconic, museum type of feel. I really stood in awe at this entire operation and how it was being run. This is what my father did for a living...sell girls into slavery, but have them sold to high class businessmen that bed them in mansions that the girls wouldn't otherwise ever have stepped foot inside of.

"Let's go. I can't wait any longer to have you," Serge slurred with that same lame faced grin painting his lips. "I have something so good waiting for you," he said, pulling my arm roughly towards him. I tried in vain to snatch my arm away from him. That just made him clamp down harder on it.

"Let me get out of the car. I can get out and walk myself. I don't need you to pull on me and push on me...for real," I grumbled, pushing him away from me. He scoffed at me, but I think he got the picture because he released his grip on me so that I could slide out on my own. Serge exited the car first and I was right behind him, but before I got out, I made a mental note of the driver's identification number and plate number for the hired car service company. The paperwork was taped to a shiny sheet on the dashboard. I thought it would be useful later. There were going to be a lot of motherfuckers going down when I got through with taking down this entire operation. I said a silent prayer that I would find Tia and be able to get the hell out of there alive, but if I didn't, I asked God to make sure that each and every one of those men, including my father, got what they deserved in the end.

CHAPTER 13

It's Real In the Field

Once Serge and I were inside of the beautiful mansion I was even more amazed at the inside. The huge expansive foyer boasted gold marble floors, at least five grandiose crystal chandeliers, silk curtains and what I recognized as priceless artwork all over the walls. There were less armed guards there than at the Maryland house where I had been prepped. That seemed strange to me because this house seemed to hold so much more value. I was looking around in pure amazement and awe when a few women that were dressed the same as the ones in the Maryland house, came out to observe and I guess take care of Serge and whatever he was going to need for his hot night with me.

"Right this way sir," one of the women said with an expressionless look on her face. "Your room awaits. Everything you asked for has been prepared. You will find that we took great care with your special requests," the woman was going on and on. Serge handed her something, she read over it and placed it at the back of a small clipboard she was holding. She looked at Serge expectantly.

"Ah yes...everything in this country is about capitalism...how much, how much, how much," Serge was saying as he dug deep into his wallet. He pulled out a one hundred dollar bill and crushed it into the woman's palm. She finally showed emotion through a halfhearted twist of her lips that I guess was supposed to be a smile. "Thank you sir. Enjoy everything and be sure to ring me if you have any problems," the woman said. When she said the word "problems" she glared at me as if she was sending me a message through her eyes. I rolled my eyes at that greedy bitch because she was no better than any of the rest of them.

Serge grabbed my hand and practically dragged me up the beautiful, red carpet covered spiral staircase. I took each step slowly, taking in a panoramic view of the rest of the house from the high perch of the steps. Something struck me like a bolt of lightening. It was a familiarity that I couldn't place at first, but then it came to me. It was so crazy because the inside of the house reminded me a lot of Tia's parent's house. So much so, that I got a strange feeling inside as I climbed up the steps. Something about that house was way too familiar for me to feel that it was a coincidence. My mind wasn't going to let go of the feelings.

Serge and I entered one of the many rooms that were at the top of the stairs.

Finally alone with you and I can hardly keep my peter in my pants," Serge joked, his British accent making the joke sound all the more stupid. When the door slammed shut behind us a cold feeling shot down my spine. He was smiling and I definitely was not.

"If you need a drink to relax you should take one now. There won't be much time for you to unwind before I have to have you," Serge continued as he shrugged out of his suit jacket and removed his tie. For some reason, I didn't have a good feeling about the entire situation. Serge was in the process of undressing and I was contemplating how the fuck I was going to keep this shit from happening. I walked over to the small wet bar and just like I had been instructed, I poured myself a whisky straight. I hardly drank and if I did it damn sure wasn't going to be whisky, but tonight, I needed something that was going to ease my on-edge nerves and give me the strength to go through with this bullshit.

"Enough with the drinking. I want you to at least be halfway alert when you feel what I have in store for you," Serge said, standing in the middle of the floor in all of his naked glory. I poured another shot of the whisky and took it straight to the head. Looking at his body told me that I was definitely going to need it.

"Take off your clothes and get on the bed and wait for me," Serge commanded. I carried the glass over to the side of the bed. I knew it was a potential weapon. Then I looked around the room for anything else that I could potentially use as a weapon in case I needed it.

"Get undressed I say! You have been defiant all night and it is starting to get on my nerves! I will call a guard if I have to!" Serge shouted, his face turning a sickening shade of hot pink. Shaking, I turned my back to him, closed my eyes and began taking off my dress. I stepped out of the borrowed heels and removed the underwear that had been put on me by those women. None of it belonged to me and right now, I felt like nothing in the world belonged to me. As I stood there, butt naked, waiting for this stranger to touch me, there was a volcano of emotions exploding inside of me. It was a mixture of pure hatred, sorrow, fear, shame and most of all the desire for revenge.

Serge rushed over to me, I could feel his presence at my back. Just his mere presence made my stomach churn in ways I hadn't felt before. I was going to be sick, I was sure of it. At first he started kissing me on the back of my neck. I closed my eyes and bit the inside of my jaw. It was all I could do to keep myself from screaming out or from turning around and punching him in the face. Next, Serge reached around to the front of me and fondled my bare breasts from behind. He was started off soft, but I could feel his touch getting rougher and more forceful with each passing minute. He was breathing hard—an animalistic pant that also made me sick to my stomach.

"You feel like magic. Your body is so beautiful. You don't seem like the type of girl that should be in a place like this," he panted into my ear. My eyes shot open. The fucking nerve of you! What type of girl do I seem like? You disgusting piece of shit! I was screaming in my head, but I didn't dare say a word. Serge kept fondling me, but then he changed from Dr. Jekyll to Mr. Hyde. His whole body movement changed as well. And within a blink of an eye, he grabbed a handful of my hair and forcefully yanked it until he succeeded in pulling me down to the floor. I was too shocked at his sudden abuse to even put up a defense or break my fall. My knees went crashing to the hardwood floors and pain shot through my legs. I felt my teeth click in the back from hitting together. The pain in my scalp from him pulling my hair gave me an instant headache.

"Ahhh!" I screamed out. I tried to put my hands on top of his to ease the pain shooting through my scalp, but Serge was too fast and too strong.

"You are my slave bitch for the night. You black bitch...you will do what I say. You do anything for me or I will have you killed. You understand me? Huh...slave," Serge growled, putting an emphasis on the word slave.

"I have a fantasy about driving my dick down the throat of a black slave. I have a fantasy about beating you and whipping you while I fuck you in the ass. I am going to live out all of my fantasies tonight," he continued, his voice sounding like a thousand snakes hissing in my ears. "Now...do what I say. Don't fight it or it will hurt worse." He said as he dragged me up off the floor by my hair. I was groaning and moaning, but to keep him from ripping my hair from my scalp I had to comply. Breathing like a raging bull, Serge tossed me onto the bed and within seconds

139

he was straddling my stomach with his body and pinning my arms to the bed with his knees. His weight felt like it was crushing my chest. I had always hated being held down. Fear of suffocation had started taking over my senses.

"Ouch! Get off of me!" I struggled, trying to buck my body and at least kick my legs. I was no match for Serge's fit and muscular body.

"Be a good girl and I won't hurt you too bad," Serge said in a tone that sounded more maniacal than he had earlier. His dick was mushy against my chest. I felt vomit creeping up from the pits of my stomach to my throat. I was afraid that if it came up I would choke to death so I fought hard to swallow it back down. It was hot and acidy. I started coughing.

"Get off of me," I gurgled.

"Shut the fuck up and don't speak unless I tell you to speak," he spat. Then he opened his hand and slapped me across my face so hard spit shot out of my mouth. I groaned and tried to kick my legs again. The anger that was welling up inside of me was threatening to explode at any second. Serge slapped me again, this time he laughed like he had enjoyed it immensely.

"Beg me to fuck you. Beg me for permission to suck my dick. Beg me slave bitch…beg me I say," he growled, looking down at me with crazed eyes. That was it. Like a damn that had broken allowing a flood, my resolve and patience had finally came apart.

"Fuck you," I croaked out. "Suck your own dick! You can't get a woman on your own so you have to buy young girls. That little sorry dick you have there ain't shit," I spat. I knew I was inciting him to be even more violent but I didn't care. I hadn't grown up to be a pushover.

Serge laughed like my words didn't even matter to him. "Ok, you want to play tough? I can play tough too," he said. He leaned over, still straddling my chest with his big body and still pinning me down with his knees and got a pair of handcuffs from the nightstand next to the bed. At first I didn't know what he'd picked up, but when I heard the metal clanking I lost it. I couldn't let him get me into a position of even more disadvantage because if I did that would be it for me.

"Don't!" I screamed. I tried to muster up all of the strength I possessed in my body to fight. I twisted my hips and tried to buck Serge off of me. Serge laughed like a crazy man and then he slapped me again.

"You can't be stronger than me. I love it when you try to fight. It just makes me even more excited," Serge growled. My nose started to bleed and the blood leaked down the sides of my face and into the back of my throat. At that moment, I looked up into his evil face and I pictured myself murdering him. I pictured myself doing something very cruel to him like removing all of his teeth one by one with a set of pliers. Right then and there I knew that one of us wasn't going to leave that room alive. If God were on my side, I would be the one leaving there with breath still in my body and not Serge.

Serge had the handcuffs dangling off of his finger with a sly smile on his face. I had to think fast if I was going to come out of this shit on top. I softened my face and swallowed hard. I had to dig deep to try and put on an act.

"Wait…wait please. Ok. Ok…I want to give you what you want. You don't need the handcuffs. Please I hate to be tied down. I will do whatever you say…just please…don't handcuff me," I pleaded softly, pretending. I spread the fakest smile over my face and looked up at Serge with big doe eyes. Serge looked at me suspiciously like he didn't know whether or not to trust me. I could tell he was contemplating what I was saying though so I kept on laying it on thick.

"Let me suck your dick. Fuck me anyway you want. You can whip me. Beat me. Burn me. Whatever you want to do to me. That is what I was born for…you know…um…to…to be your slave. But, I can't please you if you tie me up. Let me please you all night long. It's what you paid for. You can't let them get the satisfaction of not getting what you paid for. I know those crooks charged you a lot of money. I want to be worth it," I continued, using the sexiest voice I could.

"No! I want to beat you. I want to torture you. I don't want you to be so ready to serve me. I want to force you to do it. If you just give in, what fun will it be for me," Serge spat, his hair wild and his eyes evil and deranged. I was fucking shocked at his sick response. I'm sure my mouth was hanging open because I was so flabbergasted at what he just said that my mind started racing. He started to get up so he could put the handcuffs on me. That was my signal. It

142

was now or never. Ericka you're going to have to fight for your life right now. You can't let him get you. I told myself. I couldn't let him get me tied up. As soon as he eased up off of me to put the handcuffs on me I quickly lifted my knees and drove the left one right into his balls. There was no more time to be afraid; it was about survival from this moment forward.

"Aggh!" Serge screamed out, falling over on his side while holding his balls. "You little bitch!" he spat, rolling around until he was finally off of me. I scrambled up off the bed and got to my feet as quickly as I could. I was moving around and around, lost about what I would do next. That's when I looked over at the nightstand at all of the tools Serge was supposed to use to torture me. I couldn't fucking believe it. There were real rawhide cow whips, pliers, paddles, hot wax, chains, more handcuffs and two latex masks. All of that shit had been provided by Kesso's people as part of Serge's payment for the night. It wasn't like they didn't know what type of activities these clients were into.

I dove for the cow whip and at the same time Serge tried to grab me by my hair again. I swung my free arm and caught him across his face. I felt my elbow connect with the bone in the bridge of his nose.

"Aghh!" he yelled, throwing his hands up to his face. I had caught him in the right spot obviously. He stumbled backwards a few steps. The look in his eyes and the look on his face told me he was shocked. He had never expected that a captive girl would fight him back. He had been paired with his worst fucking nightmare. I wasn't done yet either.

I got the whip in my hands and squeezed it tightly so it wouldn't slip away. I eyed him evilly and let a snarl curl on my lips. I swung that fucking whip at Serge's face with all of the force in my body. The long, spiky covered spines on the whip caught Serge across his face and a few of them tangled around his neck. When the leather spines wrapped around his neck the spikes that were on them dug into his skin so far they drew blood.

"Arrgh!" he gagged and struggled, trying frantically to free himself. I yanked as hard as I could on the end of the whip, but he was too powerful for me so I couldn't get him to fall nor could I get the whip back from him. He growled and yanked on it causing me to fall. I was on the floor now, panicking as Serge struggled to free himself from the spikes digging into the veins of his neck.

"You will die bitch! You won't...get...get away with this," he gurgled, finally freeing himself. He was bleeding like crazy from the little spikes cutting him on the neck. His hands were curled into fists and his lips were drawn tightly. He looked at me with his nostrils flaring and his chest bumping up and down from breathing so hard. He squinted his eyes and zeroed in on me like a bull seeing a matador's red cape and charging for it. Before I knew it, Serge was charging forward towards me.

"Shit!" I huffed jumping aside. I whipped my head around quickly. I needed something that I could use as a weapon quick! Then, without thinking twice I picked up the lamp from the nightstand and as soon as Serge was charging in front of me, I slammed that lamp into his head. The thick porcelain lamp base shattered against Serge's head and face. I felt little sharp pains as the sprinkles of porcelain sprinkled onto my feet.

"Ahhhh," Serge let out a sickening gasp. Then he crumpled to the floor in a heap and blood spilled from a newly opened gash in his forehead. He was moaning, but he clearly couldn't move. I guess I was more powerful than I had given myself credit for. I picked up the handcuffs as quickly as I could. I grabbed his arm and handcuffed it to the leg of the bed.

"You...you...won't get away with this," he panted. "I am a very important man." I looked down at him now, bleeding and weakened.

I stood over him, naked, bleeding, sweating and breathing hard, but feeling proud of myself for not letting myself become a victim as easily as some of the other girls had. I used my foot and kicked Serge in the ribs.

"You motherfucker! You should burn in hell and you're very lucky I don't kill your fucking ass right now," I gritted and then I kicked him again. He coughed from my kick, but I knew it hadn't really done as much damage as I would've like. I looked back onto the nightstand where all of his torture tools were. I noticed a huge, black dildo, which I guess he was planning on using to evoke pain from me. I picked it up, looked at it evilly and then looked at Serge.

"I will get away with it and I will make sure all of you suffer," I gritted. Then I took the dry dildo and drove it straight into Serge's dry, tight, virgin asshole.

"AGGGGHHHHH!" he screamed out, his face filling with blood. His body bucked wildly from the pain and I could see veins cording against the skin of his neck, arms, legs and face as he strained against the pain filling his body. When the dildo was far enough in, I kicked it over and over again until I saw blood leaking from his asshole. I did it so many times, Serge finally passed out from the pain. I stood there with my chest heaving wildly as I examined my handiwork. I felt good about it too. People like him deserved much worse than I had given him.

"Oh my God!" I suddenly panicked when the gravity of the situation finally settled into my mind. I had probably killed this man with my own hands and my own will.

I was spinning around and around not knowing what to do next because it seemed like my brain just wouldn't catch up to my actions. I couldn't afford to let myself slip into shock, I had to keep it moving and find a way. The person who had taken over me and fucked that man up like that wasn't really me. It was a survival form of who I really was inside. Fighting for your life and safety sure could bring out the most primitive sides of us.

"Ericka...you have to get out of here. Ericka...mmmmm," I was whispering to myself like two separate people were there. I had to mentally keep it together. I looked over at Serge one more time. I shouldn't have, but I just couldn't help it. A huge ball of fear erupted inside of me after that and I couldn't get my bearings.

"Put on your clothes and try to get out of here. Put your clothes on and get out of here. Find a way. Find a way," I gave myself a pep talk over and over under my breath. Finally it sunk in. I was able to get it together long enough to realize that the clothes I had come there in were still where I had stepped out of them at. I rushed over to my pile of clothes and slipped back into the dress. It wasn't easy getting it zipped up enough in the back for it to stay on, but after some struggling I did it. I grabbed the heels into my hand. I wasn't trying to put them on just in case I had to move quickly once I left that room. I looked around one more time and tried to assess what I might need during an escape. All of the torture tools were too big for me to carry as a weapon inside the tiny clutch bag I had been given to carry. "Shit!" I cursed, still trying to think what I could use. There was nothing I could fashion into a weapon small enough but I was suddenly hit with an idea. Before I tried to sneak out of the room, I ran over and riffled through Serge's stuff. I dug into his suit jacket but there was nothing in it. Then I dug into his pants pockets. "Yes," I whispered to myself. There was a small folded bunch of cash. I took the cash, along with his wallet and his cell phone. Better to have something that might help me get out of here than nothing at all. I didn't know it then, but I would surely find out later that my quick thinking with taking that stuff and those few little things I had stolen were going to be my keys to freedom.

CHAPTER 14

Almost Home Free

My heart was hammering against my chest bone so hard it was moving the material of my dress. I said a quick, silent prayer as I twisted the doorknob to exit the room. Serge was still out of it and I wasn't sure if he was dead or alive at that point. I didn't care either. I was so close to freedom that I could taste it tingling the back of my throat like a nice fresh glass of cold water, which is something else I was craving at that moment. When I opened the door to the room I had been in with Serge, I didn't see anyone in the hallway, nor did I hear any voices. In fact, to me, it was eerily silent for a house that I thought should've been bustling with the sounds of the sex business. I thought for sure the men with guns would be there standing guard or roaming the hallway looking for potential escapees like me. I was wrong. There wasn't a soul visible in that hallway. I looked up and down the hallway again just to make sure my eyes and ears weren't deceiving me. It was completely silent. With my heart still racing painfully in my chest, I finally got the nerve up and stepped out into the hallway. I tiptoed towards the steps and started down them. Just as I got about three steps down a noise startled me. It was coming from the door right at the top of the stairs. I paused. I listened closely. I heard the sound of a voice. I felt like someone had just slapped me across the face when the sound came again in the form of a loud scream. The scream caused me to freeze in my tracks and pause all together. I even held my breath so that I could really decipher the sound and make sure I wasn't going crazy. I listened again just to make sure my ears weren't deceiving me. At first the sound didn't come again, so I waited. Please. Please. Please. I was chanting in my head. I needed it to come again before a guard showed up and busted me out there or one of those ladies caught a glimpse of me standing there looking crazy. Then as if God could hear my pleas the sound of the voice came again. A pang of excitement flitted through my chest and stomach. That fucking sound was music to my ears. It was unmistakable and it was like fate had put everything together. If I didn't believe it before, I sure was a believer now that God was guiding my steps through this crazy time.

Tia! I know that voice anywhere! That is Tia! Tia! I screamed inside of my head. I had been friends with Tia long enough to know her cries and her unmistakable smoky voice. I whirled around on the balls of my feet so fast I almost fell backwards down the stairs. My heart was racing so fast my head began to immediately hurt with a migraine. I followed the sound of Tia's voice to the door at the top of the steps. She had been so close all of this time, yet I felt like she was still so far away. I could feel my hands trembling fiercely as I twisted the doorknob to the room. I expected it to be locked, bolted or something. Surprisingly, the door opened with ease. I guess they weren't worried anymore about her running. Unable to control my breathing, I stepped inside the darkened room. The entire room smelled like medicine, cigarettes and stale breath. Kind of like the sick people smell. The odor hit me right in the gut and my stomach flipped. I moved a little further in and that is when I heard Tia moan and call out again.

"Help me! I need my shit! Let me out of here!" she screamed. It was definitely her. I was one hundred percent sure of it now. I swallowed hard, praying that Tia was not in really bad shape. I didn't know if I would be able to take seeing her all fucked up. I knew what these men were capable of so the thought scared the shit out of me.

"Tia?" I whispered, my lips trembling fiercely. "Tia is that really you," I said softly, my voice cracking immediately. She moaned and groaned like she was in a lot of pain. I inched forward and I could see that if it really was Tia, she had been tied up to the bed. I reached out with fiercely trembling hands and turned the button on the lamp. My eyebrows shot up into arches and my lips dropped open.

"Oh my God!" I cried out. "Oh my God! It's really you." I cried some more. I dropped the shoes I had been holding along with the cell phone and wallet that I had stolen from Serge. I fell down on top of Tia and continued sobbing like I was crazy. I was so happy to see her. The relief that I felt inside of me was so overwhelming that I could hardly catch my breath. I could only think that it had to be God's will for me to find her. There were probably a million doors in that hallway and for me to find the one door that held my best friend was just simply amazing.

"Tia...Tia it's me Ericka. Oh my God, I'm so happy to see you," I said through sobs as I tried to hug her.

"Get me out of here! Get me the fuck out of here!" Tia came alive screaming at the top of her lungs. "I need my shit right now! I need a fucking hit!"

"No! Shhh!" I jumped up and put my hands over her mouth. Tia was moaning loudly and still trying to scream. It was like she didn't recognize me or maybe she thought I was one of the women or men holding her there. Tia was bucking and screaming and I was trying to get her to shut up. She was probably high off of something or in shock. Maybe she thought she was hallucinating, which was why she wanted no parts of me. Tia continued bucking her body and fighting. That's when I noticed she had two black eyes and what appeared to be a million track marks up and down her arms. Her hair was matted and her legs were filled with huge purple, green and blue bruises. I was very surprised that those men had put up with so much from her. I assumed that Tia was very lucky that she was beautiful and exotic or else she would've been dead. I had seen Kesso's men just kill a girl in cold blood. It was unexplainable why they had left Tia alive this long with her off the chain behavior and what appeared to be a very big drug habit.

"Tia...listen to me. You have to be quiet. It's the only way I can try to get us out of here. If you scream, the men will come and we will both be caught. If they separate us again, I know I'll never see you again," I whispered forcefully in her ear.

"Ericka? Ericka is that really you?" Tia croaked. It was like the message had finally settled into her mind that I was really there. She started writhing her body frantically again. "Ericka? Is that really you?" she asked with much more urgency in her voice this time. I had to try to calm her down.

"Yes, Tia...it's me. I've never stopped looking for you. I knew I would find you. I even put myself in danger to find you Tia. I won't let anything else happen to you, I promise, but you have to be quiet now or else they'll come. If they find me here they will kill me and kill you too. You have to be quiet and let me try to come up with a plan for us," I rushed my words out so that she would really understand what we were dealing with.

"Your father...it was him. I loved him...he did this to me," she started crying.

"Shhh. I know. I know. When we get out of here, we will take care of him. But right now I need you to be strong Tia. I need to figure out how to get you out of here…to get us both out of here. These people are very dangerous and crazy. We will both be dead if we are not careful," I told her.

Tia began sobbing and shaking all over. "They did this to me. I just want to die. Just let me die," Tia cried. It broke my heart seeing her in that kind of pain. It hurt even worse knowing that my father had done this to her all in the name of fucking greed. I finally took a good look at Tia and it wasn't a pretty sight to see. I could still see remnants of her striking beauty and flawless body, but it definitely was not the same anymore. She was dangerously skinny, like they had been starving her since they took her. Her skin was ashen and dry looking. Her lips were cracked and split in several places. I could tell she had been slapped in her face and punched in her mouth. The bridge of her once perfect button nose was swollen and slightly deformed now. Her wrists had purple rings around them from being tied up and she had bruises on her thighs like they had been being pried apart day after day. All of Tia's nails were broken in jagged angles. Her toenails were chipped too. Her appearance was a far cry from her usual prim and proper, designer dressed look of the past. It was humbling to see her that way and heartbreaking at the same time.

"You're not going to die Tia. I'm going to get you out of here. Now, who put you in this room? Where is the date you were with? Did he leave? Is he coming back? Tell me Tia, I need to know everything so I can know what I'm working with," I pressed her for answers.

"No...they all keep me here for their own disgusting needs. They let the guards...the ones with the guns use me at their disposal because I...I...wouldn't be nice to the clients. They come in...all different ones...and they rape me, they beat me, they do whatever they want to me as punishment for my defiance. I almost killed the first client I was with so now the boss is making me suffer for it. I just want to die Ericka...I will never be the same ever again. They put all kinds of objects up inside of me. I am in so much pain unless they give me a hit. I need the hits to pass the time and to make it through the suffering," Tia said through tears. My insides began burning with every word she spoke out of her mouth. I don't think anything shocked me anymore, but I was still not ready to hear the things she was telling me.

"Tia...I..." I started to say, but my words were cut short.

Suddenly, I heard voices close to the door. My heart cranked up in my chest and sweat immediately broke out on my forehead.

"Oh shit!" I exclaimed, jumping up from the bed. I couldn't let them find me there or else we wouldn't get free. I looked down at Tia and she heard them coming too.

"Ericka...they're coming back. They will hurt me again. Please do something...save me Ericka...don't let them hurt me again. Please," Tia whimpered. I heard the door clicking and I was spurned into action.

"Ok..Ok..Tia…I'm going to hide. Don't tell them I am here. I will get you out of here but you have to play along," I said rushing my words out of my mouth in a whisper.

"Please…please…"she moaned. Be fucking quiet Tia! Don't let them know that I'm here or else this would all be for nothing. I was screaming inside of my head as I hurriedly ducked down and slid under the bed. She had to be smarter than that. She had made it thus far, all she had to do now was play along for a few more minutes and maybe we would be out of there. I didn't have a lot of confidence in Tia at this point. She was in drug withdrawal and she had always had a feisty personality.

I made it under the bed just in time to hear one of the armed guards walking in.

I could smell his cigarette before he was even fully in the room. It was the same guy that had sat in the corner of the room and forced me to get undressed at the other house. I already had a quest for revenge against his ass. I lay as still as I could under the bed. Tia on the other hand immediately started screaming and bucking.

"I came to see you again. I told you I would be back to finish what I had started before," the guard snarled at Tia. Then he laughed cruelly.

"No! Please! Leave me alone! I can't take anymore! Pleaaaasseee!" she screamed. Whatever he had done to her before must've been really bad because Tia was going ham knowing that he was back. It was taking everything inside of me to remain under that bed and not bolt from under it and try to fucking kill him.

"Shut the fuck up!" the guard spat. Then I heard him slap her. He laughed after he slapped her a few more times. "You junky bitch. All you want is this drug and then you'll be sucking my dick and letting me fuck you in the ass right away. I know what you like you trashy bitch. You play tough but these drugs will make you do anything," he said snidely. He laid his gun down next to the side of the bed so that he could prepare the drugs to give Tia. I peeked from under the bed and realized that I was only a few inches away from the weapon. I suddenly became extremely excited, but scared to death at the same time. I guess it was more divine intervention helping me out at that moment because I suddenly had the idea that I would be taking that fucking gun and turning the tables on this picture. I heard the guard preparing a needle full of drugs that he planned on putting into Tia's arm. I knew I couldn't let that happen or else she wouldn't be able to run when it was time for us to make our move. I had seen Tia when she was high and it wasn't a pretty picture. I couldn't chance it.

"No...don't...please stop. I don't want a hit...I don't like it anymore. Please I'll do anything, just don't," Tia pleaded. I knew in my heart that she really didn't mean it. By now, Tia was a full fledged addict and I knew she was probably craving those drugs, but she knew exactly what I knew, that if she got high she would be no good to escape. Her words spurned me into action. I reached out and grabbed the gun and pulled it under the bed.

"Shut up and stop whining. You know how I like it too so you better perform or else you know what will happen to you," the guard threatened Tia. I could see his feet move away from the bed and then they returned. I knew he was about to give her the drugs.

"Mmmm!" Tia moaned loudly. "No! I don't want it!" she screamed. That was my signal that he was probably about to stick her with the needle. I slid from under the bed with the quickness of a fucking super hero. I lifted the gun and placed it right to the guard's head.

"Leave her the fuck alone you piece of disgusting shit," I said through my teeth. "I will blow your fucking brains out if you scream, move or even try anything fucking funny and I am not fucking playing," I continued, squinting at him evilly.

"What the fuck..." he gasped, his eyes were almost bulging from his head. He was shocked as shit that he ended up on the other side of his own fucking gun. "You bitch...you won't get away with this. When the others find out they will turn you over to me and I will torture you with no fucking mercy."

"Shut up! Put your fucking hands up and don't try anything stupid or you die. I am so serious right now that you have no idea. I already want to spill your fucking brains just because of your association to this fucking business so don't try me," I spat. He shook his head in disgust but he wasn't as stupid as he looked. He did as he was told.

"Get away from her and lay down on the floor. Don't even look at her again or I will shoot both of your fucking ugly eyes out. Lay down!" I demanded, waving the gun out in front of me. I don't even know what type of gun it was, but it was huge, heavy and I knew it could do a lot of damage to whatever it hit. The guard did as he was told. I rested the tip of the gun at the base of his skull and with one hand I reached out and picked up the needle filled with the drugs from the bed where he had dropped it. My heart was beating so fast I started to feel slightly dizzy. That desperate girl inside of me was back. It was survival of the fittest at that point. I was about to take out another bastard and oddly enough, somewhere deep down inside I was craving that feeling again.

"I hope you rot in hell for the dirty shit you've done to these poor helpless girls you fucking bitch," I gritted, then I had like an outer body experience, I had turned into someone else. I bent down and plunged the needle so deep into the fat juicy vein in his neck that blood began spurting everywhere. I didn't even jump away. The blood spurted onto my legs and feet. The smell made me feel powerful. I was turning dark and evil inside.

The guard's body started shaking and convulsing fiercely. He was making a gasping sound and instinctively threw his hand up to his neck. I watched with satisfaction as he started rolling around on the floor. His movements were short lived though. I knew from the color of the blood and the frequency of how it squirted out that I had hit the artery in his neck. He didn't stand a chance. He was going to bleed to death within minutes. I loved the feeling of watching him suffer. I know it sounded evil but after everything I had been through, I had gone a little crazy inside. When his body finally went still, I reached down and got the ring of keys from his belt. The handcuff key was there and so was what appeared to be some sort of car keys.

"Yes! We are fucking getting out of here," I whispered. I rushed over to Tia and unlocked the handcuffs from her hands. Tia bolted up in the bed like she was possessed. I dropped the gun and grabbed her up into my arms.

"Please Ericka get me out of here! Don't let them hurt me anymore!" she cried out. "Please."

"I won't. I promise." I replied. I held Tia for a long time in a tight embrace. We hugged for what seemed like an eternity. I had to pull away even though I didn't want to. We were on borrowed time. Who knows how soon another guard would be coming to look for the one that was laying at my feet.

"C'mon Tia...we have to try to get out of here. You have to be real strong right now. I know you might be in a lot of pain...you've been through a lot girlie, but you have to really fight through it. If they catch us neither one of us will make it out alive. I need you to put some clothes on while I go check to see if the hallway is clear. You have to do it as fast as you can because I don't know who might be coming to look for this dude soon," I whispered. Tia shook her head up and down vigorously. She could barely walk from being kept on the bed so long but she was fighting through it. That was my girl, strong as usual. Tia found a robe that had been tossed on a chair in the corner of the room, but there were no clothes there for her. There were no shoes for her to put on either. That wasn't important in the scheme of things. They were really keeping her as a fucking hostage…no clothes, no shoes, no food…nothing but drugs and fucking abuse. That shit ate away at my heart and it was bad enough that I wanted to kill the fucking guard all over again. With a robe on, Tia walked towards me like the fucking scarecrow from the Wizard of Oz.

"My legs hurt so bad Ericka…I can barely walk. You might have to leave me here. Save yourself," Tia said with a defeated tone.

"Are you crazy? I risked too much to save you to turn back now Tia. You can do it. We can do it together," I said, trying my best to encourage her. I was so scared that she wasn't going to be able to make it down the stairs and out of that house that I felt like I would piss my pants any minute. The good thing was I had a gun now, which would definitely be a plus if I had to buy Tia some time. I was ready to shoot my way out of that fucking mansion if I had to do it. I would be spilling blood left and right if any of those guards or house women or even the clients had tried to stop me. I was on a fucking mission.

"Tia stand behind me. Stay real close to me so I can tell that you are ok. I'm going to open the door and see if I see anyone coming. Don't panic. I will give you a signal if anything is out of place out there…ok?" I whispered. My voice was shaking like shit. I don't know if I had ever been that on edge in my entire life. When your life is on the line there is no other fear that can top that. Tia listened to what I told her to do. She was so close to me I could feel her breathing on the back of my neck. Her breaths were shallow and jagged and I could tell she was petrified. I was scared as hell myself. I was playing strong right then but inside I was falling to pieces. I opened the door slowly and just as I did, I heard voices. Panicked, I jumped back and pushed Tia aside.

"Oh my God…no!" Tia cried as she stumbled backwards.

"Shit. A new group of men just came with girls. That means guards will be crawling the hallways in a few minutes. I don't know what we're going to do Tia," I said, my lips were trembling. My mind was racing.

"Ericka you can't let them get me," Tia whispered through tears. She was grabbing onto my arm with a death grip.

"I told you and I meant it, I promise that I won't leave you here," I said with sincerity. I had to stay on course with this plan that obviously was unfolding by the minute.

I clicked the lock on the door and pressed my back against it. I couldn't allow anyone to come inside. I listened to the sounds going on outside the door and said a silent prayer that they would fade soon. It seemed like forever, but finally the voices dwindled down. Tia was sitting on the floor rocking back and forth waiting to follow my lead. She looked like she was getting real sick.

"What's the matter Tia?" I asked her. She seemed like she was in pain. She was rubbing her arms frantically and moaning low.

"I am getting sick from not having the drugs. We need to hurry up or else I won't be able to move. The pain will hit my body and I won't be able to move much less run, Ericka. We have to hurry up or else I am going to die here," Tia rasped out, tears streaming down her face rapidly. I could tell she was dwindling fast. Fuck Ericka...you didn't come this far to let this happen now. I told myself. I didn't want to show my panic to Tia and make matters worse for her.

"Ok...ok...let me check out there again. One thing for sure Tia, I am not going to leave you here alone," I said with sincerity. I unlocked the door and eased it open a crack. Again, the hallway was clear, but I couldn't be sure what was going on downstairs. I breathed a quick sigh of relief to see that the hallway was once again clear.

"C'mon Tia...its now or never," I huffed. "We're going to have to make a run for it or else we might get trapped in here until another one comes."

I can't lie, my heart was beating up into my throat and adrenaline was coursing through my veins so fast it was burning in places that I couldn't describe. "Hold onto me and when I say run, Tia you will have to run."

"Ok. Ok," she said, her words coming out almost breathlessly. I could tell Tia was as scared as she had ever been in her entire life. I was playing the forceful role and I also had a gun, but truth be told, I was scared as a motherfucker.

"Ready? Tia...now! We have to do it now! Let's go!" I exclaimed. With that Tia and I bolted from the doors and ran straight for the stairs. We got halfway down before anyone was alerted to us. Then suddenly, a passing guard spotted us.

"Hey! Hey! Where are you going? What are you doing? Hey!" he shouted starting towards us with his gun. By that time we were at the bottom of the stairs.

"Run Tia...go through the doors!" I screamed.

"I won't leave you!" she replied. This was not the time for her to be defiant. I had told her to strictly listen to everything I told her to do.

"Tia, I said run! Fucking do it now!" I barked at her. Then I turned around, pointed the gun at the guard heading towards me and without even thinking twice I pulled the trigger. The gun chattered to life in my hand, but I wasn't prepared for the power that was behind the shots. The recoil sent me flying backwards. I fell hard on my ass and hit my head on the floor. The guard was down, but the loud gunshots had alerted all of the other guards and all of the guests in the rooms upstairs. Within seconds there were people running all over the house. I heard women screaming, guards yelling, and feet trampling in my direction.

I finally got my bearings and scrambled up off the floor. There was a line of cars waiting outside and

I ran straight towards them. I was running for my damn life.

"Here Ericka! Right here!" Tia yelled from the door of one of the cars. She had already climbed into one. I rushed into the car with guards hot on my heels. I pointed the gun out of the window and started shooting some more. I felt like a bad ass Rambo chick at that moment. It was an adrenaline rush that was better than any high you could get from drugs.

Tia dropped down to the floor of the car and covered her ears from the ear shattering gunshots. She was screaming and crying. "Don't let them come get me Ericka! I don't want to die! Tia was chanting over and over.

"Drive! Drive the fucking car!" I hollered at the driver. He stepped on the gas and plowed right into a guard that had gotten in front of the car to try and stop it from leaving.

"Keep driving! I don't care if you have to run over more of them! Drive!" I demanded as I showed the driver the gun I was holding.

BOOM! BOOM! BOOM!

"Aggh! Shit! Dammit! " I screamed as the sound of shattering glass cut through the car. Glass splintered all over the back seat and rained down on my head and hands. I could feel it cutting the skin on the tops of my hands as I shielded my head. The guards chasing the car had shot out the back windshield. I was very lucky that the bullets hadn't ripped through my fucking skull.

"Drive! Drive us to the nearest hospital right away!" I shouted at the driver, my voice was trembling fiercely. I held the gun on the driver just in case he wanted to get funny. When I saw the car ease onto the major highway, I lowered the gun so that I didn't attract the attention of passing cards or worse, attract the attention of the damn cops.

"Don't try anything funny or you'll die. I don't want to hurt you! I'm just trying to get my friend some help. She needs a hospital right away," I gasped out. I could feel my emotions welling up to a breaking point. I was trying to stay strong for Tia.

I helped Tia up off the floor and I held her in my arms. She was shaking like a leaf in a wild storm. Her legs were wet with piss and her teeth were chattering uncontrollably.

"We are free Tia! We are fucking free!" I exclaimed. "I am going to get you some help and everything is going to be alright. I promise that nothing is going to happen to you again Tia. Everything is going to be alright," I assured her.

"Thank you Ericka," Tia cried into my chest. "Thank you."

I felt tears welling up in the backs of my eyes but for some strange reason they wouldn't fall. I don't know how I had put my feelings aside like that, but I couldn't muster up any emotion. Not right then. Maybe later I had told myself.

Oddly enough, as much as I had just gone through in that short span of time I was calm. It was a scary kind of calm; especially because I had left two men dead back at that house. I didn't feel one bit of remorse or sorrow over it. In fact, I felt like I wanted to kill more of them. I was serene inside because I had already made up a plan in my mind. Saving Tia had been my original mission and I had accomplished that all alone. Now, I had a new mission in mind that was becoming just as important to me as saving Tia had been. I was going to destroy Kesso and his entire operation even if I had to do it single handedly without any help. I was going to confront my father and enlist his help in taking Kesso down. If my father didn't agree, then I would go about it alone. It would be his own choice after I confronted him about everything I knew. I was dead serious about this new mission. There was no way I would be able to sleep at night knowing all of those girls were still there, being held against their will, being abused by men just for shits and giggles and worst of all making Kesso and his partners wealthier and wealthier by the minute. I was going to free every single one of those girls if it was the last thing I did on earth or my fucking name wasn't Ericka Kane.

CHAPTER 15

Going For Broke

Tia was moaning and groaning like she was in a lot of pain. I think the shock of the escape might've been worse on her than anything else. Tia had been cowering and crying since we had made it out of the mansion. I felt horrible for her, but at least I could say that she was alive.

"Just hold on Tia. I am taking you to get treated. We should be there soon. This will all be over soon and before you know it…you will be back home with your parents living the good life," I comforted her. All the while my stomach was churning over and over, I was sweating and my head was pounding like someone was hitting me over it with a huge sledgehammer. I was in need of comfort myself. My nerves were rattled like a motherfucker! I was craving a cigarette and I didn't even smoke regularly. Anything that would've calmed my raggedy nerves I would've taken it at that moment.

"How much longer!" I screamed at the driver. I could hear that my own voice was quivering.

"Five or ten minutes according to the GPS," he said. His voice was quivering too. I guess if I were driving with a gun pointed at me then I'd be on edge too. As I thought about what he said it finally sunk in my brain. Shit! I didn't want him to use a GPS. The GPS would definitely track us through that shit. I knew the operation Kesso had going on was pretty sophisticated so I didn't know if that meant Kesso and his goons would be able to track the car's movements through the GPS or what. I shook my head and my stomach did another hard flip. Knowing Kesso, he had all of those cars rigged with tracking devices to keep track of where his girls were at all times after they left his possession. I could just imagine it now—guards sitting in some big room somewhere watching red dots on a map to make sure they went where they were supposed to go.

"Hold on Tia. We are almost there girl. You will be better in no time and we will be partying and hanging out again like old times," I said, rubbing her back after she let out a long wail. Kesso and his men popped back into my mind, but I shook off the thoughts real quick. I couldn't worry about that now. I needed to get Tia some treatment before the withdrawal really did her in. I had always heard that heroine withdrawal could kill a person if it wasn't monitored correctly.

ERICKA *Kane*

By the time the car screeched to a halt in front of the hospital, Tia was in full-fledged withdrawal. Her body was trembling so hard I could barely hold onto her. You would've thought she was in a deep freezer or something the way her teeth were chattering. She was writhing in pain, moaning and crying all at the same time. It was killing me to see her like that. She was a complete shell of her usual vibrant, outgoing, life-of-the-party self. I couldn't imagine the feeling of what she was going through right now, but it must've been pretty bad because Tia's cries were just getting louder and louder by the minute. I jumped out of the car and raced around to the door on her side so I could grab her out and get her inside the emergency room. My entire body was wet with sweat now. The dress I had worn on my "date" with Serge was hitched up around my hips so my ass was halfway exposed. My legs ached from all of the fighting I had done to get us out of that house. My makeup was a cakey mess and my hair was wild and crazy on my head. I'm sure I looked like a lunatic to the people watching. But I could care less. This was a life or death situation and nothing else mattered to me.

"Help! Help us!" I screamed out at the top of my lungs. "We were kidnapped and just escaped! Help us! My friend needs help!" I continued to yell out loud like I was losing my damn mind. I was screaming so hard and so loud the back of my throat started to itch and I began coughing.

"Help us! Help us now!" I went on. I could feel the blood filling up in my face. My heart thumped wildly and I was even starting to shake like Tia. I didn't even realize that I still had a death grip on that big ass gun. I must've really looked crazy. A few nurses and doctors came running outside in response to my screams, but they all started backing up when they saw the gun swinging in my hand.

"Don't just stand there! Help her!" I hollered. I was starting to cry now because things were finally sinking in. I had got myself and Tia out of the clutches of some really dangerous people. It was a big fucking deal.

"She's got a gun!" I heard one of the nurses yell out as she retreated back into the doors.

"Ma'am...it's ok. We want to help you but..." one of the doctors was saying. That's when I realized he was backing down because of the gun I was holding. I quickly tossed the gun aside.

"I don't want to hurt anyone. I just escaped from a sex trafficking ring and my friend is very sick. I need you to help her. I need you to help her before those men come looking for us. Please you don't understand...these are some very dangerous people we are dealing with," I explained, holding onto Tia so that she wouldn't hit the ground.

"Ok...Ok...let us help you and your friend. Move aside, ok. We will help her, but you have to let us do our job," the doctor was speaking slow and calm, enunciating every word slowly and loudly. He was speaking to me like I was mentally unstable. I guess in all actuality, at the moment, I was mentally unstable.

"Just help her. Don't worry about me right now. She needs the most help. She has been tied up for days, beaten, burned, raped and now she is in severe drug withdrawal from God knows what," I cried. I finally fell down to my knees and just began sobbing.

Finally two nurses approached with a wheelchair and helped Tia into it. I could hear the faint sound of police sirens wailing in the background. I didn't think I would ever say this, but, the sound of those police cars, even from a distance, was like music to my ears. It was my first signal that I was really out of the clutches of Kesso and my father for that matter. It was a sign that maybe I would be able to help all of the other girls in the end. My shoulders slumped and all of the muscles in my body went slack. Finally, I let go of it all. I let go of all of the stress, all of the fear, all of the anxiety and most of all; I let go of all of my worries for the moment. My mind, soul and body finally relaxed after days of being on high alert and in danger mode. I collapsed onto the ground outside of the hospital with a hard thud. I couldn't even feel the pain of connecting with the concrete. Nothing could compare to what I had been through, not even that. It was a combination of relief, pain, anger, hurt and exhaustion that had finally taken me down. I saw feet moving around my head and I could hear the faint sound of voices fading in and out.

"Get another chair or a stretcher! We need to treat this one too!" I heard either a doctor or nurse scream at the group that had come out to help me and Tia. That was the last thing I heard from any of them before I finally fully let go. My mind and my body just gave all the way out from the exhaustion. I reached out my hand towards the door but I couldn't hold on to my consciousness. I slipped into blackness. I didn't know if I was dead or alive.

Beep. Beep. Beep. I awoke to the sounds of hospital machines in my ears. I tried at first to open my eyes but pain shot through my head. Ugh. The worst headache I had experienced ever.

"Ms. Kane...are you awake," I heard a soft voice murmur. I thought that I was dreaming. The voice came again. When my eyes finally fluttered open, I immediately saw that the police surrounded my bed. Detective Bowles and Detective Froch were standing on either side of my bed as if they had been waiting there for me to wake up. There were about four or five uniformed officers posted up in the corners of my room as well.

"Ms. Kane...I hope you remember us," Bowles spoke up first as soon as he noticed that my eyes were open. I nodded my head slightly and even that hurt like hell. I was happy to see their familiar faces though. I did remember them from when Tia first went missing. They were the ones who had come to my house. Although at the time they were acting all suspicious of my father, and me I could respect their purpose at the time. Plus, I had no idea what I know now about Tia going missing. It was something I was ashamed of too.

"We need to ask you a few questions again. This time on your terms because we understand you've been through a lot these past few days. We were called once Ms. Cassidy was identified as the missing girl, but the doctors tell us, you were the one who brought her in. They say you said you both had been kidnapped into some sex trafficking ring? Do you feel strong enough to tell us about what happened?" Bowles rambled on. His words were swirling around in my head, but I needed to get my bearings before I spoke to them. I looked around at the hospital room. I had an intravenous line in my arm and a heart monitor on my finger. There were cops standing all around. My head felt like it had just been screwed on with metal screws and a damn hammer.

"What…what…happened to me?" I rasped out. My throat felt like I had eaten a bag of gravel when I spoke for the first time. It sounded like it too.

"We don't know. That's what we are trying to figure out, Ms. Kane. Who hurt you? Who hurt your friend Tia?" Froch replied. I could see a deep concern lacing the wrinkles on his face. His baldhead glistened with sweat too. He seemed to be just as nervous as I was. Finally it all came together. I knew what I needed to do now. I needed to tell them everything so that they could bust up the ring and save all of those poor girls. Yes! That's what I needed to do.

"I…I…think…" I started to say but my words were cut off abruptly. My eyes went wide and the heart monitors starting ringing off as my heart throttled in my chest.

ERICKA *Kane*

"Ericka! My baby girl! Oh my God! I was so worried about you! Are you all right?" My father shouted as he rushed into the room with a look of sheer panic on his face. My eyebrows went up in surprise and so did the detective's. They both whirled around, a little taken aback by my father's presence. He had always been a strong presence wherever he went so his booming voice and large built body rushing at them and me had caused the detectives and the police officers some alarm. They all moved towards my father like they were about to take him down.

"This is my daughter so you all can just back the fuck up. I got lawyers that will put you all out of fucking work and ruin your lives forever. Now, get away from her. Get away...she will not speak to you right now. How fucking dare you come and try to question her about anything while she is so weak...while she has been through so much," My father boomed. He was with two guys who stepped in and got close to the detectives. It was like a war was about to jump off right there in my hospital room. I couldn't believe my eyes. My father was definitely in a panic worried about what I was going to tell those detectives. I knew him so well.

"Wait...I want to..." I tried to say. "I need to tell...I need to tell them right away what..."

"Shhhh, Ericka! Don't speak another word! You can't trust everyone and I don't know if they will try to blame you for anything. You have to be very careful who you trust right now baby girl. I've heard so many stories on the news and on the streets.

175

Whatever it is we will discuss it when you're better. I almost died waiting to find out what had happened to you. Don't you ever scare me like that again! The most important thing right now is your health," my father huffed out. He was still trying to fucking cover his tracks. Even after all he had done and all that had happened, he was still the same person. My insides became hot and my heart monitor was screaming with beeps now. I squinted my eyes at him and pushed him away from me. He looked shocked by my sudden dismissal but I'm sure he could probably figure out by now why.

"I don't want you here! Don't tell me who I can speak to! You of all people should know about being a liar...right daddy?! You are the biggest liar and fake that I know! I know everything! I heard it from your own mouth! Oh yeah, I was there...at your office...the night after Tia went missing. You are fucking devious! I know all about what you did and what you do! I know all about who you really are! You are not Eric Kane!! You are not the father that I knew!!" I cried out. My father tried reaching down to hug me, but I just pushed him away. My heart monitors were making crazy screaming noises as my blood pressure and heart rate sped up.

"I don't ever want to see you again," I gulped out.

"Ericka don't talk crazy. You don't know anything. Things are not what they seem so don't make a mistake that you won't be able to undo later. We will work everything out when I take you home. C'mon, let's go home. I'll have my doctors come and see you. You don't have to stay here and be harassed by the police. I am the only person in the world that has your best interest in mind Ericka…you have to trust me that I know what is best," my father said, holding onto me as tightly as he could.

"Get off of me!! Get away from me!! I hate you! I hate you!" I screeched so loudly I scared myself.

"Don't do this here Ericka. It is too dangerous. You don't know what you're getting yourself into if you keep on. Don't do this. I'm begging you to listen to me for once in your life. Trust that I know everything that needs to be done to protect you," my father gritted into my ear.

"No! You are a liar!" I barked. I couldn't believe he'd go there with me. He had a fucking nerve trying to play me like that. All of my life he had been a source of comfort, but now, I didn't know what to think about him. I wanted him to hug me and comfort me, not try to shut me up with force. Tears started draining out of the sides of my eyes and pooling in my ears. My father had officially broken my heart. I didn't know if I could ever recover from the type of pain I was experiencing at his hands. He was holding onto me like it was the last time we would ever see one another. At that point, it wouldn't have been so far fetched to think that I might not ever have a relationship with him again. I was devastated inside and from how hard my father was breathing, I could tell he was devastated inside too. I am positive that he never anticipated that his business would ruin his family.

"Get away from me! I don't want to see you right now! Get away! I don't even know who you are! You are not my father...you are a monster!" I cried out as loud as I could. "You are a monster that has no regard for human life!"

As if I had pushed some magical button on his brain, my father finally released his grip on me and stood up. I was surprised and relieved at the same time. A part of me really wanted him to leave, but another part of me wished that he could stay and things could be the same for us again. My father had tears in his eyes as he took a few steps away from my bedside. He was shaking his head from left to right like I had just stabbed him in the heart with a knife. I had broken his heart, but he had broken mine first.

"Ericka...I am begging you not to do this. You won't understand until I have the chance to explain everything to you in detail. If you do this, you will not be able to go back. Come home and let me work it out with you. You don't know how much danger you are in right now. These people will not stop until they get their revenge. Even I won't be able to help you. I am begging you...let me help you now before its too late," My father said, a few tears rimming his eyes. I wanted to believe him so badly, but I didn't trust him anymore. "Ericka please," he said one last time. I swallowed hard and looked at him seriously.

"I will help all of those girls. I will destroy all of those bastards that you call business partners. I will not let them get away with what they did to me or what they did to Tia. You can either help me or you can go down with them. There are no other choices. I will not let this go. So save yourself or don't, I am going to take it all down, one piece at a time if I have to," I told my father with feeling. He looked at me with hurt and disappointment in his eyes but I didn't care. I squinted my eyes into dashes and then I slammed my finger down on the call button for the nurse. Within a few seconds two nurses came rushing back into the room. I was watching my father the entire time. I could see the pain registered on his face. I wondered at that moment could he see how much pain was registered on my face as well.

"Yes. Ms. Kane is everything ok," one of the nurses huffed, as she looked from me to my father and back again.

"No. I want this man to leave right now. He is causing me duress and I don't want him here. I want you to call those detectives back because I have information that I think will be useful for them," I said to the nurse all while keeping my eyes trained on my father. He looked at me with sorrow filling his eyes, but I could tell he had finally just given up on me. I had only seen him look at me like that one other time and that was when I had gotten myself pregnant at sixteen and had to have a secret abortion by one of his high paid doctors under gag order.

"Ericka you just made the worst mistake of your life. I can't control what will happen to you now. I am only a small fish in a very big ocean of very dangerous sharks," my father warned with an eerie finality in his tone. Then he turned and walked out of my hospital room. He stopped for a minute and locked eyes with Bowles and Froch. It was a telltale sign of what was to come and I didn't care at that time. I was about to blow the lid on my father's business and hopefully save hundreds of girls from a horrible existence. I was about to live up to the bitch with power name of Ericka Kane.

CHAPTER 16

Taking Them Down

Tia returned home after like a week in the hospital and then another thirty days in an expensive, hideaway drug rehab that her parents had paid thousands of dollars for. All of this information I had learned through the detectives. I had tried several times to reach out to Tia via telephone, email, and letters, but her parents had made sure I couldn't get in contact with her. No matter what I tried, I hadn't heard back from her. Tia was being guarded like she was the daughter of the president or some shit. I had heard that her father had paid for round the clock security wherever she went and her phone calls were being monitored by both of her parents and some high priced text and call screening service. That was just like them though, so I wasn't surprised at all. They would do all of that and blame others for anything Tia did, but they wouldn't ever admit to the fact that they had a significant role in some of Tia's shortcomings. Tia had talked to me often about how her mother and father were barely around when she was a little girl and about how she used to get into adult things from a very early age. Even when we became friends, Tia knew much more about worldly adult things than I could ever imagine at that young age.

Mr. and Mrs. Cassidy hadn't even called and thanked me for saving Tia's life. In my opinion, the ungrateful bitch had a nerve. Did she realize that if it hadn't been for me she probably would've never seen her only child again? It was cool though. I didn't need their thanks. Seeing Tia get better was all the thanks I needed. She was still my best friend no matter what I thought of her parents and what they thought of me. I had risked my own life to save Tia because I wanted to see my friend alive again. I hadn't done it for any recognition from them. Tia and I were probably never going to have the same friendship ever again, which is something that hurt me deep down inside. I had cried a few times in private over that. I mean, my father sold her into slavery, I think that would be hard for anyone to accept. I did often wonder if Tia had forgiven me and if she really wanted to see me as bad as I wanted to see her.

After I got out of the hospital I had been taken down to the police station about ten times. Now, once again, I sat across from the detectives going over things for the one-hundredth time. I drummed my fingers on the table impatiently and looked at both Froch and Bowles like they had ten heads.

"So let me ask you to go over some of the details again," Detective Froch said as he raised his hands over his head, stretched and started up with his same line of questioning again. I shook my head in disgust and let out a long breath. What wasn't sinking in? I knew he was going to go over the same damn thing again and again and again. I rolled my eyes, cocked my head to the side and listened to the same shit.

"There was a house in Maryland where they took the captive girls to clean them up, dress them and examine them? You say that if any of the girls there were what they called sick or defective they just killed them on the spot? But, none of the girls that came were brought there against their will tried to fight or run? They just let these people handle them like farm animals and they complied with everything these people asked them to do?" Froch asked in total disbelief with his eyebrows crinkled with confusion. I mean I knew that the information was kind of hard to swallow, but it was the truth and that was all I had to offer. I shook my head in the affirmative. I was growing wary of them asking me the same things over and over again. I put my fist against my cheek to show them that I was bored going over the same thing again and again.

"But then there was a beautiful mansion somewhere else, you think this mansion was in Virginia? You say that at this beautiful mansion in

Virginia, there are a gang of men with guns holding girls against their will and using them for rich clients who hold high positions in other parts of the world?" Froch went back over everything I had told them, but he formulated the information back into questions. I let out another long frustrated breath. Try to be patient Ericka. You know they are trying to trip you up to see if you're telling the truth. Just hold steady and they will get the fucking picture eventually. I told myself silently before I opened my mouth to speak again.

"I know it all sounds a little bit crazy, but I'm telling you this is what was going on. The purpose of me telling you all of this is to save those girls. There were girls on top of girls. And they are all different races. Abused and sold to the highest bidders for crazy sex fantasies. These men…the clients…knew exactly what they were paying for. They could request any type of sick fantasy and have it fulfilled. Probably shit that they could not get their wives to do at home. It was the craziest thing I have ever experienced in my life. The craziest part of it is that they run everything like it's a legitimate business. Like they are supposed to be selling young girls on an open market to be used and abused. The mansion in Virginia…the second phase of the abuse…is where I found Tia and where I was about to be tortured by some sick fuck from England that called himself Serge. The only thing that made me different from the other girls was that I didn't get snatched off the street or sold to the operation by my family. I put myself in the mix in order to save my friend. I made the ultimate sacrifice to save my best friend and now I can't even see her for five minutes to ensure that all of my hard work paid off," I said, my tone annoyed and frustrated. I could feel myself getting ready to cry and I did not want to show them any weakness right now. I needed to stay strong for myself.

Both detectives raised their eyebrows when I said I put myself in the mix. I know that they were probably calling me crazy or stupid in their minds, but I didn't think I was stupid or crazy. Either that or they really thought I was crazy enough to make up an entire story. Either way, it made me a little angry inside. I didn't like people trying to make me feel like I was going crazy or like I was lying to them. It was hard enough to be working with the cops against my father's will. I didn't need them doubting me too. I didn't need them judging me for something I did that turned out for the best anyway.

"Ok Ericka...let's just get a few things straight before we end here today. You say, these...these...foreign men, possibly from Nigeria worked for one head guy who had them bringing girls over in cargo crates through the port down in Baltimore? Just like that? Right out there in the open on the port were lines and lines of abused and kidnapped girls standing for the world to see as they were counted and herded?" Detective Froch asked me, leaning back in his chair like what I was saying was a lot to digest. I slammed my hands on the table in frustration. That was it! I had had enough of their condescending and doubtful tones. Froch and Bowles

185

both jumped because they weren't expecting my sudden outbursts of frustration. I squinted my eyes into dashes and pursed my lips.

"For the tenth time that is the truth. It's like they had everything all planned out and well worked through…like they had been doing this forever. The girls lined up but there were many cargo crates shielding them from the open view. The only reason I saw them was because I was following the men. I followed them onto their yacht. Besides that, I think everyone down at that port knows what is going on with them and why they bring girls through there, but no one would've called the police."

"Think you could help us find this place?"

"You damn right I can help you. I'll take you to the location where the girls came in right now if you want me to. I can tell you the boat where they tortured the one girl…Alicia. I saw it all with my own eyes. Everything I am saying I can verify. I just want you guys to go bust this thing up and free all of those girls. For real, I made a promise that I was not going to let them all stay there and suffer," I assured. I didn't understand why Froch wasn't getting it.

"So before I move on Ericka…let me ask you one good question," Froch said, raising his eyebrows at me suspiciously. He tapped his pen unnervingly on his writing pad. Bowles cleared his throat like he knew exactly what Froch was going to ask me. I moved to the edge of my seat waiting to hear it.

"If no one else down there was going to call the police when they saw what was going on, why didn't you call?" he asked. The question exploded in my ears like an atomic bomb. I knew at some point they were going to ask me about that. I had asked myself that several times after Tia and I had gotten rescued too. I could've just called the police once I found Serge's cell phone at that mansion and I could've hidden out until the police came. I could've called from the yacht the day I saw the girls coming out of the cargo crate. I guess there was more than one opportunity for me to call the police, but I hadn't. Would the police have even believed me if I had told them something as outlandish as what had been going on? I mean, they barely believed me right now and I had lived through it. I considered that but that wasn't why I hadn't called. I looked both detectives in their eyes and then back down at the table.

I looked into the detective's eyes and for the first time I didn't know what to say. He was right, why didn't I call the cops? Was I that fucked up in the head that I forgot to call the police? Whatever I had going on in my mind has definitely got the cops questioning me like I had a hand in the shit I rescued Tia from. If that was the case then they're sadly mistaken. And whether they realized it or not, more girls are going to be tortured and hurt really bad if they drag their feet with their rescue mission. End of story!

Although I wasn't dealing with my father, he had been gracious enough to allow me to have access to our homes and my bank accounts like nothing had ever happened. I guess there was still a slight redeeming quality about him.

I had been staying at the DC condo with Olla and round the clock police protection since I had begun cooperating with the police. I hadn't spoken to my father, but honestly, I was missing him a lot. I knew he had done some terrible things, but the more I thought about it, the more I felt like he had done them all to gain wealth so he could give me a better life since he grew up in Nigeria as a poor farmer's son. Believe it nor not, I was torn about taking down the business and being loyal to my father.

"Ms. Kane, here is your dinner," Olla said, coming into the bedroom with a tray. I sat up, a little dazed and groggy. I had been taking bunches of prescription drugs to keep my nerves at bay and to help me sleep. I was still too traumatized from my experience to fall asleep on my own.

"Thanks Olla," I rasped out, sitting up slowly. She had been so good to me since I had returned. Olla had felt responsible for everything that had happened to me because she had allowed me to leave the house when my father had told her not to. I was honestly surprised he hadn't fired her for that. I guess he recognized, as I did, that Olla was like a part of our family now and nothing was going to change that.

"I'll turn on the television for you so that you can have some company," Olla said with a small smile.

I smiled back the same way...barely. We had been being polite but I could tell she wanted to say something to me and she could tell I wasn't open to listening to her.

"Just turn it to the news," I told her. I had been making sure to watch the news everyday since I'd been back home. I don't know what I was waiting for, but I wanted to make sure I didn't miss it. Maybe I thought I would one day magically learn something about Tia from watching the news or something would come on about the police investigation into the ring.

Olla picked up the television remote, pointed it at the flat screen hanging over the fireplace and turned on the T.V.

She turned to the news channel just in time for me to see it. My eyes almost popped out of my head as I watched and listened intently.

"In breaking news happening right now, Arlington County police, Baltimore City police and the FBI have arrested forty people in what they are calling the biggest sex trafficking ring bust in United States history. Police report that the sex ring had netted traffickers over six hundred thousand dollars a week, with high priced clientele paying as much as one hundred thousand dollars for three hours with girls as young as twelve years old. Police report that it was a heartbreaking scene when they entered a house in an undisclosed location in southern Maryland, where girls were chained, beaten, given abortions against their will and even worse treated for serious medical illnesses by people who were not qualified as doctors. Police say most of the girls involved were being held against their will and sold to the ring sometimes by their own parents. Other girls were reportedly snatched off the streets of various U.S. cities never to been seen by their friends and family again. It is reported that an unknown number of girls died during their time in the house of horrors and were buried on the grounds of the property in undignified, makeshift graves dug by the men working there. The police report states that this was just one of many similar busts to come. Most recently the daughter of a prominent plastic surgeon was rescued from the same group of sex traffickers. Police will not confirm whether or not she was the person who shed some light on the dark and seedy business, but they say that they are getting very close to the heads of these operations and are confident that the entire ring will be dismantled shortly."

I could barely contain myself. The joy I felt was actually palpable. I jumped out of my bed with one big leap and hopped onto the floor. I jumped up and down like I had just found out that I had won the lottery. I was screaming and jumping like a crazy person.

"Olla! That is great news! That means some of the girls got saved! This is big news! This is awesome! Some of the girls were saved! I kept my promise! I kept my promise!" I screamed, still jumping around like I didn't have any sense. I felt so much joy that tears rained out of my eyes.

Olla had a halfhearted smile on her face and a confused gleam in her eyes. I realized then that she didn't know what the hell I was talking about. Olla had been shielded from the details of my time missing. I hadn't been able to discuss much of it with her because the detectives had warned me not to trust anyone...even Olla.

"Oh Olla...I'm sorry. You won't understand it now and it's for your own safety that I don't tell you too much...but what we just heard on the news was because of me. I was the one who saved them all...all of those girls made it out because of me. It was all because I decided that I wasn't going to just take a backseat and leave them there to suffer anymore. I promised and I kept my promise, I said proudly.

Olla smiled like she knew what I was talking about although I know she had no idea.

"Listen Ericka. I know you're happy right now, but I have to tell you something," Olla announced like she had some bad news to share. I stopped moving around, my chest was still heaving up and down, but I stood still to hear what she had to say. I looked at her expectantly.

"Your father called...he said he wants to come and see you today. He said to tell you he doesn't want to fight, he just wants to talk," Olla relayed. My eyes suddenly went dark and my mood went back to feeling down. She had fucking succeeded in killing any joy I had managed to feel from the bust.

I flopped back down on the bed and closed my eyes for a few minutes. I wanted to meet with my father, but then again I didn't. For some reason I didn't even trust him that much. What if he was just lying saying he wanted to see me so that he could lead Kesso and his people to me? I guess that was a dumb thought since my father could've just given them the address and have them come for me. Maybe he did have my best interest in mind. I was confused and I'm sure it was showing all over my face.

"Listen Ericka, he is your father and no matter what his shortcomings, he loves you. I have never seen a man love a child the way he does. I have been around you all of your life so I know how much he loves you, not just because he says it, but because of everything he does everyday to make sure that you have everything. He would give his own life for you and that I am one hundred percent sure of. I don't know everything about why you don't want to see him, but I want you to consider that he has nothing else in the world that he thinks is more important than you," Olla told me. She seemed like it was paining her to know that I wasn't speaking to my father. She just didn't know and probably could never imagine the reasons why.

Tears were welling up in my eyes because I knew she was right. I had said I would never speak to my father again after everything he had done, but Olla was right. I owed him at least one chance to really sit down with me and explain himself. He did deserve at least that much from his only daughter. Plus, I had so many questions that I needed to ask him to make sure that I could get closure inside. I contemplated everything Olla had said and everything I was already feeling. It took me a few minutes to get my thoughts together. When I finally did, I looked at Olla with tears rimming my eyes.

"Okay Olla...just for you. Tell him I will see him tomorrow. You're right, I need to hear his side of the story before I completely write him off. Besides, he is the one who had been caring for me all of my life. My other parent chose to abandon my father and I, and when she did, he never thought twice about stepping up to the plate and being a father to me. I could never repay him for the perfect life I've had so far...so for you...and for myself, I will see him tomorrow," I told her. I could see her mood lighten and I could feel a heavy burden lifting from my chest.

Olla smiled at me warmly. She looked like she wanted to grab me into an embrace, but Olla never allowed herself to have that type of contact with me anymore. She didn't want to get too attached like she was when I was a baby and a little girl. I had always wondered about that, but I had never asked her why she stopped being so close to me.

Once she left the room I started dancing around and around again. I had not forgotten that I was responsible for the bust. The rest of that fucking sex trafficking ring wasn't going to survive as long as my name was Ericka Kane. My father had said the people he worked with were very dangerous but I wasn't scared. In fact, I felt so powerful and unstoppable that I felt like I didn't even needed the police to guards outside of my condo right now. I was Ericka Kane...a bitch gaining her own power.

CHAPTER 17

Backfiring

I guess Olla had immediately delivered the message because I awoke to the sounds of a man's voice in the condo. My father came to see me the next day and I was shocked to say the least when I saw his appearance. My father was a man who took great pride in his outward appearance. He always took good care of himself and always wore the best clothes whenever he went out, even when he was just going to the store. That was far from what he was showing now. He looked skinny, tired and like he had aged ten years in the weeks since I had seen him. His shirt was extremely wrinkled, his pants looked like they could stand up by themselves and he was in bad need of a haircut.

I had my arms folded across my chest and my lips poked out, still trying to show my defiance. I was kind of happy to see him because I missed him, but I wasn't going to let him know it right away. He would have to say a lot to get me to lower my guards with him. Trust was very important to me and I felt like I couldn't trust my father still.

"Ericka," my father said, opening his arms for a hug. I think it was too much too soon. I shot him a dirty look that could've put him in the grave if looks could kill. I sidestepped away from him when he tried to move in to hug me. I wanted him to get the message that everything was not good between us right now. He was going to have to explain a lot of shit before I just let him act like everything was fine.

"Daddy, let's not pretend that everything is good and that nothing has happened between us," I started, my tone forceful and firm. "You have a lot of explaining to do. I am so confused about who you are. I just want to know why? I want to know how you…a man with a daughter…could participate in something like that, even if it was in the name of making money," I told him. I felt a lump forming in my throat and tears welling in the backs of my eyes. I didn't want to cry and make myself look weak, but he was my father still and I loved him.

"Ericka when you were born you were the greatest gift God had ever given me. Growing up I always thought I was cursed to live like a pauper all of my life. When I came to the US and I was offered the job to just oversee things with the business I took it. It was the most money I had ever made. Then I met your mother there. She was one of the captive girls, but I saw something in her. I fell in love and I rescued her. When you were conceived it was out of love. But they made her turn on us. They threatened to kill us if she didn't go and be with the boss of the operation. She sacrificed herself for us and I had lost all of my dignity. At that point, I didn't care anymore about anything except making sure nothing like that ever happened to you. I had to give them Tia or else they said they would kill you or snatch you into the business. They were constantly threatening you and I," my father said, he was sobbing like I had never seen a man cry before. I was crying too because I had no idea about any of that.

"How can I believe anything you tell me? You lied so much of my life that I don't even know what to believe. I don't even know if you are who you say you are," I said through sobs. My father finally wrapped his arms around me.

"Because I just wouldn't lie about something like that. It is all said and done now. There is no reason for me to keep lying," he said sincerely.

I threw my arms around his waist and melted into his embrace. I cried like I was at someone's funeral. In a sense, I guess I was at a funeral burying the unknown and the hurt and pain my father and I had both suffered.

"I'm sorry daddy," I cried.

"For what?" he asked.

"For cooperating with the police. And for not trusting you," I cried some more. I felt so vulnerable at that moment. He was probably the only person in the world who could do that to me.

196

"It was going to happen one day anyway. Nothing lasts forever. But now, we have to leave Ericka. With this latest news these people won't rest. They are extremely dangerous and they don't like to be crossed. They have been requesting that I turn you over to them, but I won't. I told them I won't," my father said, his tone was serious but I could hear the fear underlying his words.

"I don't want to run. I want to be around to see each and every one of them go down. I can't run now," I replied.

"Ericka then you must prepare yourself for what might come. You must prepare yourself to die," he said seriously.

I looked at him strangely and for the first time in a long time I could tell that my father was serious. Not only was he serious, he was scared down to the core of his being.

BANG! BANG! BANG! I jumped out of my sleep to ear shattering booms. I fell off the side of the bed, that's how scared I was when I heard the noises. I was sure it was gunshots that I was hearing. Another round of loud bangs and Olla's screams told me what I needed to know.

"Daddy?!" I called out as I scrambled up off the floor. I didn't get an answer. I could hear the sound of feet trampling outside of my bedroom door. It sounded like a herd of elephants were stampeding through the condo. My father had decided to stay the night in his room, so my heart was hammering in my chest wondering if he was ok. I ran to my door to lock it, but before I could fully turn the doorknob the door splintered open.

"Ahh!" I screamed out as shards of the door burst into my face knocking me backwards onto the floor.

"Get that bitch!" I heard a man's voice boom. When I heard that accent my entire body got hot like someone had set me afire.

"No!" I screeched and tried to run. I was no match for the number of men that had flooded into my room. It was clear that I was their main target. I was still going to fight to the death. I couldn't stop fighting now. I lunged forward for the lamp on my nightstand, but I wasn't fast enough. One of the men grabbed me by the back of my nightgown and dragged me back down to the floor.

"He wants her and the father brought in alive so don't kill her," One man told the other.

"Get the fuck off of me!" I growled, kicking my legs. I was sure I caught the one holding me a few times. Then when he went down holding his balls I knew I had succeeded. It was all for nothing though because another one just pounced on me like a damn lion on a gazelle.

This one punched me in the face. "Uh," I let out a winded breath. I was stunned into submission. He had hit me in the face so hard I heard something crack and I was literally seeing the little squirming stars. I could feel my face swelling up within seconds. I had no more fight in me. That hit had taken the wind and the energy right out of me.

"Let's go. It won't be long before the police sends the change of shift officers and they will know what is going on," one of the men said. I wondered how they had even gotten past the cops on duty outside of my condo without alarming them.

"Agggh!" I screamed as one of the men hoisted me into the air and threw me over his shoulder. "Stop fucking moving and don't fucking scream again or you die," another man said, stepping close to me and putting the end of his gun in my face.

"Where is my father?" I barked. "I want to see my father and make sure he is alright," I said and I tried to kick and punch.

"Ericka," I heard my father say once we were in the living room of the condo.

"Daddy! Are you ok?" I called out.

"Just do what they ask Ericka. I will do my best to save you," he said.

"Shut the fuck up!" one of the men yelled, then he took the end of his gun and drove it down on my father's head.

"Agghh! Don't hurt him!" I belted out.

"Where is the lady that was here?" the man holding me asked the other. Just then I heard Olla's cries.

"Oh my God! Olla!!! Leave her alone!!" I cried out. Then I looked over and saw that they had Olla down on her knees and turned away from them.

"Please! Don't! Don't hurt her…" I started.

BOOM! BOOM! BOOM!

I gulped the rest of my words down my throat. I opened my mouth to scream but no sound came out as I watched Olla's head just explode from three powerful gunshots.

"Olla!!!!!!" I hollered. Her body dropped forward with a sickening thud and there was more blood than I had ever seen in my life. I could see her brain hanging from her skull by a few bouncing threads of muscle and membranes.

I started gagging. "I'm going to be sick. I have to throw up!" I told the man carrying me. He dropped me like I was a poisonous snake. I landed on my back with a hard crash to the hardwood floors of the DC condo. My ears were ringing and pain shot through the back of my head like someone was hitting me with a hammer. I rolled onto my side and threw up.

"Ericka are you ok?" My father asked. I couldn't even answer him. Of course I wasn't ok. I was being fucking kidnapped for real this time. Olla was innocent in all of this and now she was dead.

"Let's go. This is taking way too long," one of the men announced. All of the other men seemed to fall in line. A different man scooped me up off of the floor like a rag doll. I knew once they removed me from my condo that I was doomed. Not only I was doomed, I also had a strong feeling that my father was going to suffer the same fate as I was.

"Get off of me! Get the fuck off of me! You won't get away with this!" I screamed. One of the men rushed over and cracked me in the face with his gun. That surely shut me up. I don't think I had ever felt that kind of pain. I was dazed into silence as they exited the condo with me. Through blurred vision I saw the two police officers that had been guarding my condo door. Both of them had been shot in the head, their bodies slumped against the wall outside of our door. I watched as the men pushed my father out of the condo at gunpoint. I could only pray that Froch and Bowles would figure out that their officers were dead and come looking for me. I thought I had done a good enough job of helping them uncover even more of Kesso's spots. Now all I could do was pray for the miracle that the raids they were planning for today would save my father's lives and me.

CHAPTER 18

The Beginning of the End

My naked body shivered as my blood ran down my face, chest and stomach. I couldn't stop my legs from shaking and I felt like my bladder would explode at any moment. Wherever they had me, it was literally freezing cold like I was naked in Alaska.

"Hit her again," a man's voice boomed. I braced myself because I knew exactly what was coming next. "Please," I whispered, but that was for nothing. It was clear that these very dangerous people were not going to have any mercy on my soul or me. It was also clear to me that if I ever got out of here, I would hunt down each and every one of them and torture them ten times worse.

"Agggh!" I let out another scream as I felt the shock waves from the oversized stun gun that was being used to torture me. It had to be something they use on large farm animals to make them submissive. I didn't know how many more high-powered surges of electricity my body would be able to take.

My face was scrunched up and my eyes rolled into the back of my head. Sweat was pouring from every pore on my body. I gagged but nothing came up from my stomach. I was in so much pain I felt like even the organs inside of my body hurt. My heart pounded painfully against my weakened chest bone and my stomach literally churned. I was wishing for death because even that had to be better than what I was feeling at that moment. Another hit with the electric current caused piss to spill from my bladder and splash on the feet of one of my tormentors.

"This bitch pissed on me!" he growled. Then he took his huge hand and slapped me across the face so hard spit shot out of my mouth.

"Daddy! Help me!" I struggled to get the words out as my body jerked fiercely from another hit from the stun gun.

"Please let her go," my father mumbled, his words coming out labored and almost breathless. "Just take me, but let her go," he whispered through his battered lips. I had heard him coughing and wheezing as our captors beat him unmercifully. It was almost unreal what we were going through. As hard as the torture was, it was even harder to see my father in a position of total helplessness. He had always been my hero all of my life. When my mother decided that she didn't want to be a mother anymore, it had been my father who'd made all of the sacrifices to take care of me alone. He was always so strong and heroic to me, but now, he was just as weak and useless as me.

"Daddy," I panted, my head hanging. "Don't let them kill me."

I squinted through my battered eyes and tried to see him, but the bright lights my torturers were using prevented me from catching a real good glimpse of my father. I figured that I would probably never see him again. I could hear the voices around me clearly though, so I knew we were all in close proximity.

"You betrayed us, Eric. You and your little bitch daughter here thought you could outsmart us. I should have never trusted you as a business partner. I should have known that such a weak man, who would run from his native country, would give in to these American ideals. You were once a son of Nigeria...a man who loved his country, now a traitor, a betrayer, and a weak pussy. You got too big for yourself. I knew when you came to this country that you would think you were the boss of everything. I let you have a good life here. Yes, you were living in a big mansion, rubbing elbows with the wealthy white Americans that you wish you could call your brothers, and most of all working with the police to bite the hand that feeds you," Kesso, who I now recognized as the tall, ugly, man with black skin and yellow eyes, hissed as he came into focus in my vision. He had stepped around the bright light and I could see every feature of his hideous face. He resembled a Gorilla because there was something grotesque about his features. His nostrils were almost non-existent and those little beady eyes didn't look like they belonged on a human face at all.

"No. I did everything you asked, Kesso. I was always loyal to you, my entire country and my fellow Nigerians. I helped all of the people you sent to me. I gave them jobs. I gave them money. I gave them places to stay. I repaid my debts to you over and over again. I entered into this business unwillingly, but I did it to repay the debts I owed you for helping me get to America. I turned over everything you asked for...including all of the slaves you wanted. All of the money you wanted. You even took the only woman that I ever truly loved from me. What more could I do, Kesso? Now, you have my daughter," my father cried as another round of punches landed in his midsection. More cracks and coughs came as the men pounded on my father, breaking bones and injuring his insides. I heard my father's words, but I couldn't believe my ears. Did my mother run to my father's business partner? Did my father get into something that he would never be able to get out of? It was a lot to handle because I had always worshipped the ground that my father walked upon. My heart was breaking watching him suffer. It was worse than any pain my torturers could impose on me right then.

"Daddy! Stop hurting my Daddy!" It was killing me to know he was in all of that pain. After I discovered what my father was into I was devastated, but that didn't change the fact that I loved him and that he was all that I had in the world. I recognized that the position we were in right at that moment was my fault too. My father had pleaded with me to leave the situation alone. He had asked me to stop investigating and to stop trying to dig up the truth. My father had actually pleaded with me to just accept everything the way it was, but I couldn't do it. He knew how stubborn I could be, but there was nothing much he could do about it. I had to keep investigating for myself. I had to call in the assistance of the police. I wanted justice! That was the stubbornness in me that I had gotten from my mother. She was the type of bitch that never backed down from something that she wanted. As much as I hated her, I was like her in a lot of ways…all of her bad ways. Now, my father and I were facing death with no clear way out of the situation. All because of me! If anyone deserved to die, it was me.

"Daddy I'm so sorry! I just wanted to help. I just wanted to make things better. I just needed some answers. I never meant to have this happen to you. I told you Kesso! Just kill me and let my father go! It is me that you want! I was the one who brought all of the heat to your door and pulled the lid off of your business! It was all me…not my father!" I cried some more. I bet this so-called African prince wasn't used to a woman speaking to him like that. I hated him and I didn't care about any traditions.

"Shut her up! I'm tired of her fucking mouth. This little bitch cost me millions of dollars because she wanted to play Nancy Drew…now I want to see her suffer. She's a piece of shit just like her father. She is not worth sharing the same air with," Kesso, the ugly man barked, waving his hands. His goons immediately surrounded me. My heart rattled in my chest, but there was nothing else they could do to me that would hurt me more than the possibility of my father dying at my hands. I gave up at that moment. Whatever was going to happen must've been our fate from the beginning, I reasoned with myself. I kept screaming things that I knew were disrespectful in the eyes of my father's Nigerian counterparts. I wasn't going to be one of those passive women. No! I knew what those bastards were doing to women and I could only hope that the call I had made before they snatched me would help me in the end.

After a few minutes, one of those huge, wrestler type dudes grabbed me by my hair and dragged me across the gravel floor. "Agh!" I screamed. It was like nothing I had ever felt before. I don't know how after all of those hours of torture, I didn't slip into shock. My entire body felt like someone had doused me with gasoline and lit me on fire. I could feel the once perfect skin on my legs and ass shedding away against the rough floor. I didn't want to die, but if I was going to die, I was going to go out fighting. I tucked my bottom lip under my top teeth and gritted.

"Get off of me! Get the fuck off of me!" I screeched so loudly my throat itched. "Fuck all of you! You're all going to burn in hell for what you're doing!" I continued; feeling blood rushing to places on my body that I didn't know even existed. I bucked my body wildly, but all of my fighting efforts were to no avail. Of course they were stronger than me. Of course I wasn't going to be able to break free, but it just made me feel slightly better inside to try. I never dreamed of going out of this life on my feet. My father always called me his little African lion and I planned to live up to that name before I died. The man dragging me finally roughly let go of the fist full of my hair he had been holding. He released me with so much force that my head slammed to the floor. I felt something at the base of my skull come loose. I was dazed for a few seconds, but not for long. I was brought back to reality when I felt a boot slam into my ribs. The force was so great that a mouthful of blood spurted from my mouth.

"You don't have such a big mouth now, huh?" the goon hissed, his accent thick and barely understandable.

"Please don't hurt her anymore. I will give you everything I have if you just let her go," I heard my father gurgle.

"It is too late for that. You and your little troublemaker should've thought about that before both of you betrayed me. Now, someone has to pay with their life. There will be no more talking," Kesso said with finality. The next thing I heard was the ear-shattering explosion of a gun.

"No!!!!!" I belted out, right before my entire world fell apart. Blackness engulfed me and I wondered how it had all come to this. Not even a month ago, my father and I had been so happy. Now I was dead. This time as I moved towards a bright light, I was sure that I was dead.

"Ericka! Ericka! Can you hear me! Ericka! Stay with us! Don't slip away! Stay with us!" I heard someone screaming at me as I came back into consciousness. "Get me a IV drip and a tube right away. She has internal bleeding and we need to get some of the blood out of the chest cavity before she drowns on her own blood," the voice yelled. I had to force myself to stay awake. I didn't know where I was, but it was like some unknown force was pulling me in one direction and I was pulling in the opposite direction.

"C'mon Ericka! You're strong enough to make it. C'mon girl," that same voice was screaming. "Tube! Slats!"

When my eyes finally opened there were blinding bright lights above me and people running around me frantically. I could hear the blip of the monitors and suddenly I was aware of the severe pain pulsating through my entire body. I moved my eyes to the side and noticed the nurses dressed in their scrubs. I was back in the hospital, that much I could see, which meant that Kesso and his people were no longer torturing me. I had been saved, but I had no idea by whom or how. I thought for sure I was going to die there. I started thinking about my father, but I didn't have enough strength to ask if he had made it. I wondered if whoever saved me had also saved him. I closed my eyes and prayed that my father was still alive.

"Is she going to make it? I need to know! We need her to be protected! She is important to us…you have to work as hard as you can to save her!" I heard the familiar voice of detective Froch saying. He was in a panic. "We didn't save her from those bastards for her to die here. Make sure you save her life. I don't care what you have to do, but you have to save her," Froch said with feeling.

With that, I closed my eyes and let the doctors do their job. I was still alive and so was my will to live. I was going to make it because I wanted to and because obviously God had some plan for my life. Kesso had not succeeded in killing me. He could not break me the first time, nor could he kill me this time. It was evident that I was better and more powerful than he was. He used other people to be strong, but me, I only had myself to thank for everything that I had overcome. The doctors continued to work on me but they seemed a little less frantic.

"She is starting to stabilize. I don't know what we did or what happened, but her vitals are improving by the minute," the doctor said to his team.

"Maybe it was just God. Maybe it wasn't her time. Maybe there is some greater purpose for her life," one of the nurses replied.

"Yea…maybe you're right," the doctor acquiesced. I had to agree. It wasn't my time. Right there on that table as the doctors and nurses rushed to save my life, I vowed to myself to go after Kesso and his people with a vengeance they have never experienced. Even if Kesso was dead or in police custody right now there

would be others following in his footsteps. It was my mission to take the power from them and save the girls. I was definitely planning to live up to the name Ericka Kane. They had better get ready for me...a bitch with power was born right there in that hospital room once they decided to save my life. I will be back. I will be better. I will be the baddest bitch anyone had ever laid eyes on. Me...Ericka Kane!